Spoken English
A Foundation Course
for speakers of Marathi

Part 1

Kamlesh Sadanand
Formerly, Professor and Head
Centre for Phonetics and Spoken English
CIEFL, Hyderabad

Susheela Punitha
Formerly, Professor of English
Mount Carmel College, Bangalore

Voices on CD
S Upendran

Aakash Chakrabarty
Shanti Balasubramaniam
Parvathy Raveendran
Gayatri Pillai
Kamlesh Sadanand
Prema Naraynen
Sirish Kumar

Orient BlackSwan

ORIENT BLACKSWAN PRIVATE LIMITED

Registered Office
3-6-752 Himayatnagar, Hyderabad 500 029 (A.P.), (INDIA)
email : centraloffice@orientblackswan.com

Other Offices
Bangalore, Bhopal, Bhubaneshwar, Chennai,
Ernakulam, Guwahati, Hyderabad, Jaipur, Kolkata,
Lucknow, Mumbai, New Delhi, Patna

Content developed by
Tata Learning Solutions and Educational Services Private Limited

First published by Orient Longman Pvt. Ltd. 2008
First Orient Blackswan impression 2009

Cover & book design

ISBN 13 : 978 81 250 3465 0
ISBN 10 : 81 250 3465 X

Typeset in Zap/Ellipt BT 12/14 by
OSDATA
Hyderabad 500 029

Printed in India at
Sujata Printers
Mumbai 400 013.

Published by
Orient Blackswan Private Limited
R. Kamani Marg, Mumbai - 400 001.
email : mumbai@orientblackswan.com

Contents

Module 1

1. Meeting People, Exchanging Greetings and Taking Leave 1
2. Introducing Yourself 7
3. Introducing People to Others 11
4. Giving Personal Information 18
5. Talking about People, Animals and Places 21

Module 2

6. Answering the Telephone and Asking for Someone 31
7. Dealing with a Wrong Number 37
8. Taking and Leaving Messages 41
9. Making Inquiries on the Phone 46
10. Calling for Help in an Emergency 52

Module 3

11. Getting People's Attention and Interrupting 57
12. Giving Instructions and Seeking Clarifications 62
13. Making Requests and Responding to Requests 71
14. Asking for Directions and Giving Directions 81
15. Thanking Someone and Responding to Thanks 88

Module 4

16. Inviting, and Accepting and Refusing an Invitation 97
17. Apologising and Responding to an Apology 112
18. Congratulating and Responding to Congratulations 119
19. Paying Compliments, Showing Appreciation, Offering Encouragement and Responding to them 124
20. Asking for, Giving and Refusing Permission 135

Module 5

21. Talking about the Weather 145
22. Describing Daily Routines 155
23. Talking about Possessions 163
24. Talking about Current Activities 170
25. Asking for the Time and Date 176

Appendices

Appendix A: Distinguishing between Spelling and Sound 183
Appendix B: The Consonants of English 187
Appendix C: The Vowels of English 191
Appendix D: The Relationship between Spelling and Sound 195
Answer Key 201

Foreword

The importance of English, both as an international language and as a link language, is now widely accepted. It is also well known that students belonging to the rural areas have problems in learning and speaking English. Recognising this urgent need, the Department of Intermediate Education, Government of Andhra Pradesh, has for some time been focusing on the teaching and learning of English with particular reference to rural students. With the upswing in economic activities and with the service sector booming in the country, there is an explosion of opportunities available to persons at different levels of competence and skills. All that is required is the added advantage of the ability to communicate effectively in English. This is the main reason behind starting a short-term course in spoken English in government junior colleges. It is a known fact that students in rural and semi-urban areas do not have adequate exposure to spoken English and that there are not many institutions which can impart training. Hence, the Department of Intermediate Education has taken on a pilot project to conduct spoken English courses in select government junior colleges to train students in oral communication.

An effective training programme will prepare students for job interviews, will elevate their confidence levels and enable them to use English whenever the situation demands. For this, they need practice in speaking that starts them with the basics and takes them to an advanced level through carefully guided activities. Proficiency in oral communication also needs an exhaustive and systematic practise of the micro-skills of listening and speaking. The language inputs that are necessary include essential vocabulary, grammar and functions of English. To make listening interesting, it is useful to have stories, jokes, puzzles, jumbles, songs and anecdotes in the text to motivate the students to be active learners. Role play and dialogues based on day-to-day interaction make the listening and speaking interesting. As the course progresses, it will be necessary to train students to understand the meaning of words through contexts without the frequent use of the dictionary. Similarly, they will need to understand newspaper captions, relate them to different social issues and use them to debate on these.

I hope that the course in spoken English prepared by experts in the field and by practising teachers fulfils the requirements of average students and relates to their sociocultural backgrounds. I also hope that the course, the outcome of a joint project undertaken by the Department of Intermediate Education and Orient Longman, will become part of the regular curriculum, attracting and benefiting many students in the long run. I am sure that the principals and the faculty members in the colleges where the course is being offered will involve themselves wholeheartedly in this programme and ensure its success.

D Chakrapani, IAS
Commissioner of Intermediate Education, A.P.

PREFACE

Traditionally, the term 'spoken English' meant pronunciation and most courses in spoken English, therefore, focused on teaching it. The present course is different in that it does not concentrate on pronunciation alone but integrates all aspects of the spoken idiom, that is, grammar, pronunciation and social appropriateness. The aim of this course is to help students develop their oral communication skills in English. It is intended to help those students who have had a regional language as the medium of instruction at school and who have had little or no exposure to spoken English.

Given, that there is an increasing demand for proficient speakers of English in the context of the increasing importance of oral communication for employment, this course attempts to help students at the intermediate and undergraduate levels enter the mainstream and compete with those who have had English as the medium of instruction. Keeping our learner in mind, we have drawn extensively upon our knowledge and experience of first-language learning in designing the materials. Thus the materials include:

- *Listening:* A child's continuous and constant exposure to a contextualised use of his/her language is an essential input to the language learning process. We have thus included an extensive listening component in this course to give our learner as much exposure to contextualised use of English as possible.
- *Production:* The production of language by children is at first limited to imitation of contextualised language used by those around them. This helps them to internalise language and later confidently extend it to other socioculturally similar contexts. We hope that the activities requiring the student to repeat the samples of simulated dialogues they listen to will help them learn socially appropriate language and later extend its use to situations in everyday life.
- *Extension:* The activities that follow the listening and repetition of dialogues are intended to help the learner extend the use of appropriate language for various communicative functions to similar sociocultural contexts. In order to do this the learners write their own dialogues in a given context and enact them.

The course comprises 11 modules. These have fifty communicative functions in all. The functions range from those that require fixed formulaic expressions in conversation (e.g., greeting, introducing, telling the time, making inquiries, etc.), and are therefore easy for the learner to acquire, and those that require the use of more complex structures and are consequently more challenging (e.g., persuading and dissuading, describing events, states and habits in the past, explaining words and actions, giving reasons, expressing intentions and purpose, expressing possibility, obligation and necessity, etc).

While we expect that the first five modules will enable students gain the confidence necessary for fluency, we hope that the later modules will help them develop greater accuracy in oral communication.

Last, but not least, in Module 11 we draw the student's attention to the need for the use of the dictionary for help with the pronunciation of English words. To this end, we have designed tasks that will sensitise student to the difference between spelling and sound, help them learn the consonant and vowel symbols and the sounds they represent, and to pronounce words as transcribed in the dictionary and to transcribe words as pronounced. On the whole, we have endeavoured to prepare materials that are self-instructional and learner friendly.

Kamlesh Sadanand
Susheela Punitha

To the Student

If you wish to speak English well in different situations which you might find yourself in, you will find this course very useful. The dialogues in each unit exemplify a range of situations in which you may want use English to communicate with others and you can listen to these on the accompanying CD. The activities in each unit are intended to help you acquire the essential features of conversational English. In order to fully benefit from the course you must

- listen carefully to the conversations in each limit on the CD;
- imitate those conversations by repeating them;
- learn the words/phrases/expressions used to express different functions by using them in the conversations you write as part of the activities in each unit;
- make sure you will be able to use the words/phrases/expressions outside the classroom by enacting the dialogues you have written;
- not be afraid of making mistakes initially for as you advance you will become much more fluent and confident;
- use only English to communicate with your classmates in the classroom;
- request the teacher to play the CD again if you find an activity difficult;
- take help from your partner or the members of your group when necessary;
- practise using the expressions you have learnt in similar situations outside the class room.

To the Teacher

To facilitate learning of the spoken idiom, teachers would need to

- plan to complete each unit in no less than two hours;
- go through each unit carefully *before* meeting their class and make a note of the communicative function to be taught;
- listen to the recording that accompanies the text;
- be prepared to play the recording of conversations more than once if the students so desire;
- play the CD for the answers to each activity only *after* the students have completed it;
- ensure active participation in the activities by moving round the class;
- help the slow and shy learners gain confidence by ensuring that each group has one or two confident students;
- allow students to prompt each other and correct their peers;
- let students know that after they complete a group activity that requires pair work, they must share their responses with the group to which they belong;
- encourage students to communicate in English as long as they are in class;
- step in to help correct students only when it is absolutely necessary, that is, when students are unable to solve a problem in spite of all their efforts.

Acknowledgements

This book owes its publication in the short time it was done to the following persons at Orient Longman, who stepped beyond the limits of duty and gave, generously and without hesitation, of their time, thoughts and skills to help in the completion of the project.

Planning and coordination	:	Mr B M M Ali and Mr Tapan Das
Production	:	Mr Girish S Mondkar and Mr V Murali Krishna
Project facilitators	:	Mr S K A Murali Mohan Rao, Mr N Manikandan, Ms B Rajya Lakshmi and Ms Y Sujatha
Marathi translation	:	Ms Pratibha Gopujkar
Typesetting and illustrations	:	Ms Ch Susheela and Mr M Nayab
Voices for the audio-CD	:	Mr Aakash Chakrabarty, Ms Prema Naraynen Ms Parvathy Raveendran and Ms Gayatri Pillai
Editorial department	:	Dr Devi Gopalakrishnan

MODULE 1

UNIT 1

MEETING PEOPLE, EXCHANGING GREETINGS AND TAKING LEAVE

It is important to know how to use English to greet people politely when we meet them and to end the conversation when we take leave of them. The way this is done is slightly different in formal situations (when you are talking to a person whom you do not know very well, to a very senior person, to your teacher or your boss, for example) and in informal situations (when the person you are speaking to is a friend or a relative).

लोक भेटल्यावर सभ्यपणे त्यांचे स्वागत कसे करावयाचे व निरोप घेताना त्यांच्याशी काय बोलायचे हे माहीत असणे महत्त्वाचे आहे. औपचारिक प्रसंगी (उदाहरणार्थ, काहीशा अनोळखी व्यक्तीशी, अत्यंत ज्येष्ठ व्यक्तीशी, तुमच्या शिक्षकांशी किंवा ज्येष्ठ सहकाऱ्याशी बोलताना) आणि अनौपचारिक प्रसंगी (तुम्ही बोलत असलेली व्यक्ती मित्र किंवा नातेवाईक असेल तर) हे संभाषण थोड्या वेगळ्या पद्धतीने करावयाचे असते.

Listen to a formal dialogue between two persons and follow the dialogue in the book. You can use the words in bold when you need to greet someone in English or to end a conversation.

DIALOGUE 1 (FORMAL)

(Gita Naidu and Madhu Kumar meet at the post office. They stay in the same colony, but do not know each other very well. It's three o'clock in the afternoon.)

Madhu : **Good afternoon**, Mrs Naidu.

Gita : **Good afternoon**, Mr Kumar. **How are you?**

Madhu : **I'm very well, thank you. And how're you**, Mrs Naidu?

Gita : **I'm fine, thanks**. I came to buy some stamps and inland letters.

Madhu : I must send this card to my friend. It's her birthday next week. **Have a nice day**, Mrs Naidu.

Gita : **Thanks**, and **you too. Bye!**

Madhu : **Goodbye!**

ACTIVITY 1

Listen to the dialogue again and repeat each line.

Useful points to remember

1. Specific

   The two persons in the dialogue you listened to are neighbours, but they do not know each other very well. So, (a) they address each other by their titles, not by their first names: *Mrs Naidu*, not *Gita*, and never *Mrs Gita*, and (b) they say *Good afternoon* to greet each other, not *Hello* or *Hi*.

2. General

   ✎ When we talk, we usually say *I'm. . .*, *It's. . .*, *How're* ... instead of *I am ..., It is ..., How are ...* .

   ✎ We usually say *Good morning* up to twelve o'clock midday, *Good afternoon* between midday and five o'clock in the evening, and *Good evening* after five. We never say *Good night* to greet a person.

   ✎ Make sure to say *Bye* or *Goodbye* like the speakers you heard on the CD, with the voice moving from low to high.

PAIR WORK

ACTIVITY 2

Take turns to enact the roles of Mr Kumar and Mrs Naidu with a partner.

Listen to an informal dialogue between two persons and follow the dialogue in the book.

DIALOGUE 2 (INFORMAL)

(Lakshman and Srinivas are good friends. They meet outside a restaurant after a month.)

Srinivas : **Hello**, Lakshman!

Lakshman : **Hi**, Seenu! **I haven't seen you for a long time. Where were you?**

Srinivas : **I was busy in** school practising for Sports Day. I was in the races.

Lakshman : How wonderful! You must've won many prizes.

Srinivas : Not many. Only three.

Lakshman : That's great, Seenu. Congratulations!

Srinivas : Thanks. **And what have you been doing? Come, let's** have some coffee. **We haven't met in a long time.**

Lakshman : **Wish I could have stayed, but** I'm really late for college. Let's meet on Sunday.

Srinivas : We'll do that. **Bye, bye**!

Lakshman : **See you**!

Useful points to remember

1. Specific

   Lakshman and Srinivas know each other very well. So:

   - Srinivas addresses Lakshman by his first name.
   - Sometimes we call our friends by their pet names, just as Lakshman addresses Srinivas by his pet name, *Seenu*.
   - They say *Hello* and *Hi* to greet each other, not *Good morning* or *Good afternoon*.

- They say *Thanks* instead of *Thank you*.

2. General

When speaking, we say:

- *haven't* for *have not*
- *that's* for *that is*
- *we're* for *we are*

ACTIVITY 3

Listen to the dialogue again and repeat each line.

PAIR WORK

ACTIVITY 4

Take turns to enact the roles of Lakshman and Srinivas with a partner.

ACTIVITY 5

a. Complete the following dialogue. After you finish, listen to the dialogue on CD and enact it with a partner.

(Shankar Rao meets Mohan Reddy, who has recently moved in as his neighbour.)

Shankar Rao : Good morning, Mr Reddy. How ....?
Mohan Reddy : Very well, ... you. How ...., Mr Rao?
Shankar Rao : I'm .... We're happy to have you as our neighbour. Do come home sometime.
Mohan Reddy : We certainly will. Thank ..... . See you then.
Shankar Rao : ....

Note that we say *Mr Rao*, not *Mr Shankar*.

b. From the two expressions in brackets, choose one that would be suitable in informal spoken English and fill in the blanks in the dialogue. After you finish, listen to the dialogue on CD and practise it with a partner.

(Manju meets her friend Parvati after school, and they walk home together.)

Manju : Hi, Parvati! Are you in the play for Parents' Day?

Parvati : Hi, Manju! No, our class is presenting a group song. .... a Gujarati folk song. (It is /It's)

Manju : Wonderful! ..... glad. You have a great voice. (I am / I'm)

Parvati : .... What's your class doing? (Thank you / Thanks)

Manju : .... doing, 'Bhima and Bakasura.' I'm Kunti. (We're / We are)

Parvati : Then, ... have to wear a sari, won't you? (you will /you'll)

Manju : ...., I hope I can manage that. (Yes / No)

Parvati : Oh, you will. .... worry. (Do not / Don't)

Manju : ...., Parvati. Bye. (Thanks / Thank you)

Parvati : .... (Goodbye / Bye)

Activity 6

Mr Kumar meets Ms Raman, his son's teacher, at the school. Write a dialogue between them, using the outline below.

- Mr Kumar greets Ms Raman.
- Ms Raman returns the greeting and asks him how his son, Kiran, is.
- Mr Kumar says that Kiran is much better but that he has to rest for a week.
- Ms Raman says she hopes Kiran will get well soon.
- Mr Kumar thanks her.
- They take leave of each other.

Activity 7

Enact the conversation you have written with a partner.

Activity 8

Listen to the following conversation and enact it with a partner.

(Radha goes to Lata's house. They talk about what they will wear for Lata's brother's wedding.)

Lata : Hi, Radha! Come in. I was hoping you'd come today.

Radha : Hi! I came to ask you what you'll be wearing for your brother's wedding.

Lata : I'll be wearing a new red skirt with a green blouse. And what're you wearing, Radha?

Radha : I'll be wearing the blue sari I got for my sister's wedding.

Lata : How lovely! That's such a beautiful sari. We'll have a great time together.

Radha : Yes, we will.

Note that we don't say *we'll* at the end of a sentence.

ACTIVITY 9

Work in pairs. Write a dialogue based on the following guidelines and enact it. (You can change items b–d.)

a. Exchange greetings.
b. Ask your partner about what happened in office that day. (You were on leave and did not attend office.)
c. She/he tells you that it was a quiet day at the office. The director left for Kolkata.
d. Thank her and say you will be in office the next day.
e. Take leave of each other.

MODULE 1

UNIT 2

INTRODUCING YOURSELF

This unit will help you learn how to say who you are after greeting someone who does not know you. You will also learn how to respond to introductions. There are different ways of doing this depending on whether the situation is a formal or an informal one.

अपरिचित व्यक्तीचे स्वागत केल्यानंतर आपली ओळख कशी करून द्यावयाची हे या पाठात तुम्ही शिकणार आहात. कोणाशी ओळख झाल्यावर काय बोलायचे हेही तुम्ही शिकणार आहात. प्रसंग औपचारिक आहे की अनौपचारिक यानुसार वेगवेगळ्या पद्धतीने हे संभाषण करावयाचे असते.

a Introducing yourself to someone

Listen to the following dialogue and follow it in the book, noting which parts of it are spoken with more force than the others.

DIALOGUE 1 (FORMAL)

(Prakash Reddy is a new teacher. He introduces himself to the headmistress, Nina Shetty. Time: morning)

Prakash Reddy : **Good morning**, Mrs Shetty. **I'm** Prakash Reddy. **I'm** the new history teacher reporting for duty.

Mrs Nina Shetty : **Good morning,** Prakash. **(I'm) pleased to meet you.** Welcome to the National School. **We're glad to have you.**
Prakash Reddy : **Thank you. I'm looking forward to working here.**

ACTIVITY 1

Listen again to the above dialogue and repeat each sentence aloud.

Listen to the following dialogue and follow it in the book, noting which parts of it are spoken with more force than the others.

DIALOGUE 2 (INFORMAL)

(John is at a party. He introduces himself to Ahmed, his brother's friend.)

John : Hello. **I'm** John. **I'm** Joseph's brother.
Ahmed : Hello, John! **Nice to meet you.**
John : **Nice meeting you too.**

ACTIVITY 2

Listen again to the above dialogue and repeat each sentence aloud.

b Two strangers introducing themselves to each other

Listen to the following dialogue and follow it in the book, noting which parts of it are spoken with more force than the others.

Dialogue 3 (Formal)

(Two scientists meet at a seminar. Time: afternoon)

Dr Swamy : **Good afternoon! I'm** Narayana Swamy **from** REC, Warangal.

Dr Rao : **Pleased to meet you,** Dr Swamy. **I'm** Srinivas Rao **from** Nehru Technical University.

Dr Swamy : **I'm so glad to meet you.** Will you be presenting a paper today?

Dr Rao : Yes, it's a report on my latest project.

Dr Swamy : **That's interesting.** I'm looking forward to your paper.

Dr Rao : Thank you.

Activity 3

Listen again to the above dialogue and repeat each sentence aloud.

Other ways of introducing yourself are:

Let me introduce myself. I'm ....
I'll introduce myself. I'm ....

Activity 4

Fill in the blanks after each greeting by introducing yourself in different ways. Say each item aloud for practice.

a. Good morning, ma'am. ....
b. Hello. ....
c. Hi. ....

Activity 5

Fill in the blanks after each greeting by introducing yourself in different ways. Say each item aloud for practice.

a. Excuse me, Mr Das. ....
b. Hello, Kala. ....
c. Hi, Babu. ....

PAIR WORK

ACTIVITY 6

Use the expressions you learned in this unit to fill in the second line in the dialogues below. Enact the completed dialogues with a partner.

a. *A*: Hi. I'm Paul Vincent. Please call me Paul.
B: ....

b. *A*: Hello. My name's Abdul Anees.
B: ....

c. *A*: Hi. I'm Sheila, Ajay's cousin.
B: ....

MODULE 1

UNIT 3

INTRODUCING PEOPLE TO OTHERS

This is closely related to what you learned in unit 2. In this unit, you will practise how to use English to introduce two persons who are strangers to each other. Again, the language you will use to do this will differ depending on whether the situation is a formal or an informal one.

दुसऱ्या पाठात तुम्ही जे शिकलात त्याच्याशी याचा खूप जवळचा संबंध आहे. एकमेकांना न ओळखणाऱ्या दोन व्यक्तींची ओळख इंग्लिशमध्ये कशी करून द्यावयाची याचा तुम्ही या पाठात सराव करणार आहात. अर्थात, भाषेचा वापर औपचारिक व अनौपचारिक प्रसंगांमध्ये वेगळा राहणार आहे.

Listen to the following dialogue and follow it in the book, noting which parts of it are spoken with more force than the others.

DIALOGUE 1 (FORMAL)

(Mrs Nina Shetty introduces Mr Prakash Reddy to Mr Akash Yadav, the English teacher.)

Mrs Shetty : Akash, **I'd like to introduce** Mr Prakash Reddy to you. He's the new history teacher.

Akash Yadav : **Hello**, Prakash. **Glad to meet you.** I'm Akash Yadav. I teach English.

Prakash Reddy : **Nice to meet you too.**

ACTIVITY 1

Listen again to the above dialogue and repeat each sentence aloud.

Listen to the following dialogue and follow it in the book, noting which parts of it are spoken with more force than the others.

DIALOGUE 2 (INFORMAL)

(Vijay, who is with his sister Kamala, meets his colleague Sagar at the railway station. He introduces the two.)

Vijay : **Hi**, Sagar. Going home to Guntur, are you?

Sagar : **Hi**. Yes, I'm taking the Chennai Express.

Vijay : Sagar, **meet** my sister Kamala. Kamala, **this is** my colleague Sagar. **He's** just become the head of our accounts department.

Kamala : **That's nice. Pleased to meet you**, Sagar.

Sagar : **Nice to meet you too.**

ACTIVITY 2

Listen again to the above dialogue and repeat each sentence aloud.

Now, listen to some more dialogues and follow them in the book.

DIALOGUE 3 (FORMAL)

(Dr Rekha Gupta and Mr Sriram Kumar are guests at the annual day function of a college. They do not know each other, but both of them know the principal, Dr Kiran Murthy. Dr Murthy introduces Dr Gupta to Mr Kumar.)

Dr Murthy : *(to Mr Kumar)* **Mr Kumar, meet Dr Rekha Gupta**. She's the new member on our Board of Governors. (*to Dr Gupta*) **Dr Gupta, (this is) Mr Sriram Kumar**, **the secretary**.

Mr Kumar : **Good morning, (Dr Gupta). I'm pleased to meet you.**

Dr Gupta : **Good morning. I'm pleased to meet you too.**

Mr Kumar : We're glad you agreed to be on the board.
Dr Gupta : It was kind of you to ask me.

DIALOGUE 4 (FORMAL)

(Mrs Nina Shetty, the principal of a school, introduces Mr Prakash Reddy and Mr Akash Yadav to each other.)

Nina Shetty : (*to Prakash Reddy*) Prakash, **here's** Mr Akash Yadav. **He** teaches English. (*to Akash Yadav*) Akash, **I'd like to introduce** Mr Prakash Reddy to you. **He's** the new history teacher.

Akash Yadav : **Hello**, Prakash. **Glad to meet you.**

Prakash Reddy : **Nice to meet you too.**

DIALOGUE 5 (FORMAL)

(Shashi introduces her professor Dr Prakasam to her friend, Amit Dutta, who has been admitted to the first year BA class.)

Shashi : Amit, **I'd like you to meet** my professor, Dr Prakasam. Sir, **this is** my friend, Amit Dutta. **He's** taken the BA English course.

Dr Prakasam : **Pleased to meet you**, Amit.

Amit : **I'd heard so much about you**, sir. **I was eager to meet you.**

Dr Prakasam : **Thank you. That's kind of you. I hope you enjoy** your studies here.

Amit : **I'm looking forward to** attending your classes, sir.

Dr Prakasam : **I'll see you** in class tomorrow then.

Amit : Yes, sir. I'll be there.

Look at some other expressions you can use to introduce people to one another.

I'd like you to meet...............

Have you met?

Do you know each other?

Let me introduce ....

May I introduce ...(formal)

It gives me great pleasure to introduce .... (to an audience at a public function)

Useful points to remember

In formal situations:

- A woman is introduced to a man.
- If the persons being introduced are both either women or men, then the older person is usually introduced to the younger.
- At the work place, the senior person is introduced to the junior.

ACTIVITY 3

Listen again carefully to each of the conversations and repeat them. You can follow the lines in your book.

GROUP WORK

ACTIVITY 4

Form yourselves into groups of three. Each group can choose one of the dialogues above for practice. Take turns to enact your dialogue until every member of the group gets a chance to be the person who introduces as well as a person being introduced.

ACTIVITY 5

The following conversation is incomplete. Fill in the missing lines and enact the dialogue with the others in your group.

(Bhat introduces his boss Mr Deepak Dhanraj to the social worker Mrs Vimala Lal.)

Bhat : Mr Dhanraj, ... She is a .... *(to Mrs Lal)* Mrs Lal, ... Mr Dhanraj is ....

Mr Dhanraj : Hello. Pleased.. .

Mrs Lal : I'm .... too.

Mr Dhanraj : I really appreciate the work you've been doing in the city's orphanages.

Mrs Lal : Thank you. It's kind of you to say that.

ACTIVITY 6

Write a conversation in which you introduce your mathematics teacher to your father. Say that your teacher makes mathematics very interesting. Enact the dialogue in groups of three.

Listen to the dialogues below and follow them in the book.

DIALOGUE 6 (INFORMAL)

(Sheila and Praveen are classmates. They meet at an exhibition. Praveen is with his cousin, Ranjit, whom Sheila has never met. Praveen introduces Sheila and Ranjit to each other.)

Praveen : **Hello**, Sheila! Ranji, **this is** Sheila. **She's** in my class. Sheila, **meet my cousin**, Ranjit.

Sheila : **Hi**, Ranjit. Nice meeting you!

Ranjit : **Hi! Nice meeting you too**, Sheila! **You can call me** Ranji. Praveen has been talking about you.

Sheila : Hope he's been saying nice things about me. D'you[1.6] like the exhibition?

Ranjit : Yes, very much. We're yet to get to the food stalls.

Sheila : Go along then. The dosas are great.

Praveen : We'll go and try them. Bye then!

Sheila : *(to Praveen)* Bye! See you tomorrow. (*to Ranjit*) Bye, Ranji. See you!

[1.6] the shortened form of 'do you', used in spoken English

DIALOGUE 7 (INFORMAL)

(Arun and Ravi are neighbours. They go to the playground to play cricket. Their friend, Prakash, joins them. He has come with his neighbour, Dinesh. Prakash introduces Dinesh to Arun and Ravi.)

Prakash : **Hi**, you two!

Arun and Ravi : **Hi**, Prakash!

Prakash : (to Arun and Ravi) **Meet** Dinesh. **He's my** neighbour. **He's in** his college cricket team. *(to Dinesh)* Dinesh, my friends Arun and Ravi.

Dinesh : **Hi**, (both of you)!

Arun : **Hi**, Dinesh!

Ravi : **Hi. Glad to have you here.**

Dinesh : **Thanks.**

ACTIVITY 7

Listen again carefully to each of the conversations and repeat them. You can follow the lines in your book.

GROUP WORK

ACTIVITY 8

Form groups of four. Take turns to introduce any two members of your group to the third person.

Note that in conversations, we use the following shortened forms of words.

I'm	*for*	I am
you're	*for*	you are
he's	*for*	he is *or* he has

she's	*for*	she is *or* she has
we're	*for*	we are
they're	*for*	they are
I've	*for*	I have
you've	*for*	you have
we've	*for*	we have
they've	*for*	they have
d'you ...?	*for*	do you....?
what's....?	*for*	what is....?
where's....?	*for*	where is...?
when's.....?	*for*	when is....?
how's....?	*for*	how is...?
who's...?	*for*	who is...? *or* who has. . . ?

PAIR WORK

Activity 9

Write down the expressions we use to introduce and to respond to introductions in both formal and informal situations. Practise saying them with your partner.

Introductions	*Responses*

MODULE 1

UNIT 4

GIVING PERSONAL INFORMATION

Sometimes when you introduce yourselves, you also need to give some personal information, such as your age, where you stay or belong to, your family and educational background and what you are doing. In this unit, you will learn how to do this in both formal and informal situations.

आपली ओळख करून देताना कधीकधी आपल्याबद्दल वैयक्तिक स्वरूपाची माहिती द्यावी लागते, जसे आपले वय, आपण कोठे राहतो किंवा आपले गाव, आपले कुटुंब आणि आपले शिक्षण तसेच आपण काय करीत आहोत. औपचारिक व अनौपचारिक प्रसंगी हे कसे करायचे ते तुम्ही या पाठात शिकणार आहात.

Listen twice to the dialogue below and follow it in the book.

SELF-INTRODUCTION 1 (FORMAL)

(It is the first day of college for the first year BSc students. Each student has been asked to introduce herself / himself to the teacher and the class, and to give personal information. Listen carefully to what Surya Kumar says. Time: 11 a.m.)

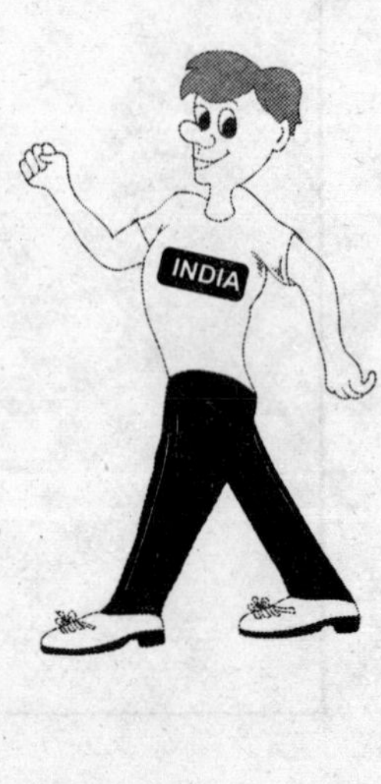

Good morning to all of you.

I'm Surya Kumar. **I'm** eighteen. **I come from** a small village in Kurnool district. Most of the people in the village are farmers. **My father** is also a farmer. **My mother** looks after the home. **I have** two elder sisters and one elder brother. **I'm** the youngest in the family. **My sisters are** both married. One lives in Hyderabad and the other in Bangalore. **My brother is** doing his engineering. **I went to** a government school in Kurnool and passed the Intermediate examination with a first class. **I would like** to do my MBA after graduation. **I love** playing kho kho and football. **I'm fond of** music, mainly film songs. **I like** drawing too. **I'm looking forward to** making many friends here.

To introduce himself and give some bits of personal information, Surya Kumar does the following:

- Begins by greeting everyone.
- Then he tells them
  - his name and age
  - about his hometown
  - about his family
  - about his schooling
  - what he would like to do
  - what his hobbies / interests are.
- Ends by saying how it feels to be in the college.

Activity 1

Here are some other expressions you can use in such a situation. Listen to them carefully and repeat them aloud for practice.

a. Good morning everyone.
b. My name is…
c. I'm … years old.
d. My home town is …
e. I studied in …
f. I plan to …
g. My hobbies are… / I'm fond of … / I'm interested in …
h. I'm delighted to be … / I'm happy to be . . .

Listen twice to the dialogue below and follow it in the book.

SELF-INTRODUCTION 2 (INFORMAL)

(Saira Begum talks to her new classmates during the lunch break and tells them about herself. Listen carefully to what she says.)

> **Hi! I'm** Saira. **I'm** seventeen. **I'm from** Hyderabad. **I live near** the Charminar.
>
> **My father's** a cloth merchant. **He has** a shop near Madina Hotel. **He sells** readymade garments. If you're interested in buying clothes, I can take you to my father's store. **My mother teaches** in a nursery school. **She's a** wonderful cook. You can come home anytime because she loves to cook for our friends. **My brother's** in high school. **He's** very naughty, but we're good friends. **Both of us love to** watch movies on TV. **What else can I say about myself?** Oh, yes. **I'm fond of** painting. So, if any of you is interested, I can paint a picture of you. **I'm so glad** to be here. **I'm sure** we'll have a great time together.

Note that we say *father's* instead of *father is* and *brother's* for *brother is* when speaking.

GROUP WORK

ACTIVITY 2

Form groups of four or five and take turns to introduce yourselves to the others in your group and to give personal information. You can use formal or informal expressions.

MODULE 1

UNIT 5 TALKING ABOUT PEOPLE, ANIMALS AND PLACES

a Describing people

When we describe people we usually say what they look like. We can talk about their face, their hair, their height and weight, and the clothes they are wearing. (Later in the course, we will also learn to say what people do, where they live, what they like, etc.)

लोकांचे वर्णन करताना साधारणपणे ते कसे दिसतात हे आपण सांगतो, त्यांचा चेहरा, केस, उंची आणि वजन, आणि त्यांनी घातलेले कपडे यांविषयी बोलतो. (हे लोक काय करतात, कोठे राहतात, त्यांना काय आवडते याविषयी आपण या अभ्यासक्रमात नंतर शिकणार आहोत.)

Here is a picture of Ramesh Babu's family. He is with his wife, Savitri, and their children Savita and Raghu. Listen to the description of Ramesh Babu on CD and follow it in the book.

DESCRIPTION

Ramesh Babu's **tall and big-built. He has a long face with a hooked nose. He has a fine moustache. His hair's black and straight. He has small eyes. He's wearing a white dhoti and kurta.**

GROUP WORK

ACTIVITY 1

a. Form groups of ten and take turns to describe Savitri, Savita and Raghu to the others in your group. Use some of the expressions in the box below.

tall and plump	tall and big-built
short and slim	tall and thin
straight hair	black hair
curly hair	wavy hair
long plait	long hair
short hair	thick hair
fine moustache	short beard
long face	oval face
large eyes	small eyes
wide mouth	small mouth
round face	big ears
broad forehead	long nose
hooked nose	sharp nose
small nose	thin lips
salwar kameez	pointed chin
plain sari and printed blouse	white dhoti and kurta
white pants and black T-shirt	long skirt and short blouse

b. Listen to the descriptions of Savitri, Savita and Raghu on CD and compare them with yours. Then listen again to each line and repeat it aloud.

ACTIVITY 2

Take turns to describe any one person in your group, using the clues in brackets. Write out the description first and then speak. The person you describe should stand up at the end of the description.

His/her ....'s .... (name) . He/she .... (height/ weight). He/she.........has .... (hair/eyes/face). He/she .... (sings, paints,etc.) well.

ACTIVITY 3

Think of a person in your group. Complete your responses to the questions below about the person with words such as those in brackets. The others in the group will then ask you these questions to guess whom you have thought of.

a. How tall is the person?
   She/he's ....(tall, short, of medium height)
b. Can you describe the person's hair?
   It's .... (wavy, curly, straight, long, short)
c. What is the colour of the person's eyes?
   They're .... (black, brown, grey)
d. How is the person dressed?
   He/she's wearing .... (jeans, shirt, skirt, blouse, T-shirt, pants, salwar kameez)

ACTIVITY 4

Write two sentences each about any two members of your family. After everyone in the group has finished the task, take turns to say aloud what you have written in the blank spaces below.

a. ....

   ....

b. ....

   ....

PAIR WORK

ACTIVITY 5

Work in pairs. Fill in the line that Raju's father says to describe his friend and enact the dialogue with a partner, taking turns to play each of the two roles.

Father : Raju, my friend will be coming by the 10 o'clock bus from Warangal. Can you meet him at the bus stop and bring him home, please. I have to go to the office urgently.

Raju : I'll be happy to do that, Father. But how will I find him? I haven't seen him.

Father : ....

Raju : Does he have a moustache?

Father : No, he doesn't, but he wears glasses.

Raju : I think I should now be able to recognise him. Don't worry, Father. I'll bring him home.

Father : Thanks, Raju.

Raju : You're welcome.

b Describing animals

How would you talk about animals to others? You can tell them what they are called, what they look like, what they eat and where they live.

प्राण्यांविषयी तुम्ही इतरांशी कसे बोलाल ? प्राण्यांना काय म्हणतात, ते कसे दिसतात, काय खातात आणि कोठे राहतात यांविषयी तुम्ही इतरांना सांगू शकाल.

Listen to two people talk about a dog and follow the dialogue in the book.

DIALOGUE 1

Maria : Hello, Salim! How're you?

Salim : Hello, Maria. I'm fine, thank you. How are things with you?

Maria : I'm okay. Hey, is that your pet dog?

Salim : That's right. **He's a** Labrador. **I call him** Munna. **He's just** three months **old**.

Maria : I love his **brown coat.** And **he's so soft and cuddly!**

Salim : **He's very friendly too.**

Maria : What do you give him to eat?

Salim : Well, mainly milk. He also **loves** rice and meat cooked together.

Maria : Where does he sleep?

Salim : **On a** soft rug in the corner of my bedroom.

Maria : I must come home and play with him sometime.

Salim : Sure. That'll be nice.

ACTIVITY 6

Listen to the lines again (recorded with pauses between each) and repeat them for practice.

ACTIVITY 7

Look at the numbered pictures of animals. Choose from the words in the box and fill in the blanks in the dialogue. The first one is done for you as an example.

bear	buffalo	camel	cow	deer	donkey
elephant	giraffe	goat	lion	monkey	tiger

A: What d'you see in picture 1?

B: It's a lion.

A: What's there in picture 2?

B: That's a ....

A: What's the animal in picture 3?

B: It's a ....

A: What d'you see in picture 4?
B: There's a ....
A: Could you describe the animal in picture 5, please.
B: It's a ....
A: Tell me about the animal in picture 6, please.
B: It's a ....
A: What does picture 7 show?
B: A ....
A: What d'you see in picture 8?
B: It's a ....
A: Describe the animal in picture 9, please.
B: It's an ....
A: What d'you see in picture 10?
B: A ....
A: Could you name the animal in picture 11, please.
B: It's a ....
A: What's there in picture 12?
B: That's a ....

ACTIVITY 8

To check your answers, listen to the above questions and answers on the CD. Note carefully how the names of the animals are pronounced. Repeat the answers for practice.

PAIR WORK

ACTIVITY 9

a. Work in pairs. Take turns to talk about the animals in the list below, using the given expressions. For e.g., look at the description of a lion.

The lion looks like a huge cat. It has a mane around its face and neck, and grey or green eyes. It has long whiskers. The tip of its tail is bushy.

lion	:	looks like a huge cat; has a mane around its face and neck, grey/green eyes and long whiskers; tip of its tail is bushy
tiger	:	looks like a large cat; has black and yellow stripes
giraffe	:	has a very long neck and long, thin legs, and large spots on its body
monkey	:	has a long tail
donkey	:	looks like a horse, but is smaller; has long ears
deer	:	has spots on its skin, gentle eyes
bear	:	has thick fur on its body and a big snout
camel	:	a tall animal with a hump on its back, and long legs with padded paws
elephant	:	a huge animal with big, fan-like ears, tiny eyes, a long trunk, tusks and legs like pillars
cow	:	has short horns and a long tail
buffalo	:	big and black, looks like a cow, has long curved horns

goat : not very big, has horns on top of its head

rabbit : a small animal, has long ears and soft fur

zebra : an animal like a donkey, but with black and white stripes

b. Listen to a speaker talk about the animals on CD, and repeat the sentences for practice.

GROUP WORK

ACTIVITY 10

Get into groups of 10. Members of the group will take turns to call out the name of an animal. The member who raises his/her hand first will stand up and describe the animal in two or three sentences. If the person is able to do this well, he/she gets a point. If the description is not clear or is incorrect, the other members can try, and whoever gives a satisfactory description gets two points. The activity can continue until every member gets a chance to call out names of animals. You can choose any animal, not necessarily those in the pictures. You can use the kinds of sentences below to help you talk about the animals.

The .... is ....

It has ....

It is found mainly in ....

C Describing places

When you want to describe a place to someone, you can talk about where it is and how big it is, and also say what it has and how it looks, etc.

तुम्ही एखाद्या जागेचे वर्णन करून कोणाला सांगू इच्छिता तेव्हा तुम्ही ती जागा कोठे आहे आणि किती मोठी आहे हे सांगू शकता तसेच तिथे काय आहे आणि ती कशी दिसते हेही सांगू शकता.

Listen to the dialogue on CD in which a person describes her house to a friend.

DIALOGUE 2

Smita : Farida, I heard you have moved into a new place. Where is it?

Farida : **It's not very far from** college, **just to the left of** the Amar theatre. **It's a two-room flat.**

Smita : That's nice! What's it like?

Farida : It's **bright and airy**. There are **large cupboards** in both the rooms and **two open balconies.**

Smita : You seem happy.

Farida : I am. The flat's **very comfortable**.

Smita : I'll drop in next weekend if I can.

Farida : Please do. You're always welcome.

ACTIVITY 11

Listen again to what Farida says about her new flat and repeat the sentences aloud.

ACTIVITY 12

Write down answers to the following questions in the blank spaces. You can use any of the given clues, or you can give your own answer.

1. Where are you from?

   ....

   (a big city, a small town, a village)

2. How would you describe your village or hometown?

   ....

   (noisy, dusty, crowded, peaceful, an industrial town, has many high-rise buildings, on the banks of a river, has farms, has green fields, has small houses)

3. What is it famous for?

   ....

   (weavers cooperatives, small-scale industries, historical monuments, multinational corporations, an old temple/church/mosque, wooden toys, a clean beach)

GROUP WORK

ACTIVITY 13

Use your answers in Activity 12 to tell your group about the place you come from. You can begin your sentences with *It's... / There are ... / It has... .*

PAIR WORK

ACTIVITY 14

Listen to the dialogue and enact it with a partner.

Somu : Hello, Shiva! What're you planning to do during the summer vacation?

Shiva : I'm going to my grandfather's village with my parents. Why don't you come along with us?

Somu : I'm not sure if I'd like to go to a village, Shiva.

Shiva : But why? We can have a lot of fun. There's a river flowing by the village. We can go swimming. We can also climb trees. There are many fruit trees in the garden. I have a lot of fun whenever we visit my grandfather. Come with me, Somu. We'll have a great time.

Somu : Sounds exciting! Let me ask my parents. Bye.

Shiva : Bye.

MODULE 2

UNIT 6 ANSWERING THE TELEPHONE AND ASKING FOR SOMEONE

The telephone is very much a part of our lives today. In this unit you will learn to use English to make a telephone call, answer the telephone, greet the person at the other end of the line, ask for someone and respond when someone else makes such a request. You will also see how the language of formal telephone calls is a little different from that of informal calls.

आपल्या आजच्या जीवनात दूरध्वनीला महत्त्वाचे स्थान आहे. इंग्लिश भाषेतून दूरध्वनीवर संपर्क कसा साधावा, आलेला दूरध्वनी कसा घ्यावा, दुसऱ्या टोकाला असलेल्या व्यक्तीचे स्वागत कसे करावे, दुसऱ्या व्यक्तीला फोन देण्यास कसे सांगावे व अशीच विनंती समोरून आल्यास काय उत्तर द्यावे हे या पाठात तुम्ही शिकणार आहात. औपचारिक आणि अनौपचारिक दूरध्वनीमधील भाषेत फरक कसा करायचा हेही तुम्ही पाहाल.

Listen carefully to the formal telephone conversations below and follow them in the book.

DIALOGUE 1 (FORMAL)

(The phone rings in the office of EduBooks Publishing Company.)

Receptionist : **Good afternoon. EduBooks Publishing Company.**

Caller : **Could I speak to** the sales manager, please.

Receptionist : **Could I tell him who's calling, please.**

Caller : **My name's Nitya Menon. I am calling from the Women's College library.**

Receptionist : **Thank you,** ma'am. **I'll put you through to** Mr Abdullah, the sales manager.

Caller : **Thank you.**

DIALOGUE 2(FORMAL)

(The phone rings in Suman's home.)

Suman : **Hello. Suman Bhushan.**

Caller : **Hello. Could I speak to Mr Prem Bhushan, please?**

Suman : **May I know who's calling?**

Caller : **I'm** Srinath, his colleague.

Suman : **Hold the line, please. Mr Bhushan will talk to you in a moment.**

Caller : **Thank you.**

DIALOGUE 3 (FORMAL)

(The phone rings in Ms Samuel's home. Santosh takes the call.)

Santosh : **Hello, this is 27613625.**

Caller : **Is that** Ms Karuna Samuel's residence?

Santosh : **Yes. Would you like to speak to her?**

Caller : **Yes, please.**

Santosh : **Could you hold on a minute, please. I'll call her.**

Caller : **Thanks.**

Listen carefully to two informal telephone conversations below and follow them in the book.

DIALOGUE 4 (INFORMAL)

(The phone rings in Sitara's home.)

Sitara : **Hello.**

Caller : **Hi,** Sitara, **This is** Arun.

Sitara : **Hi,** Arun. **What's up?** (informal way of saying, *What's happening?*)

Caller : **Nothing much**. Remember, we have a meeting tomorrow morning.

Sitara : Thanks for reminding me, Arun. It's about the editorial for the school magazine, isn't it?

Caller : Yes. Just wanted to make sure you'll be there.

Sitara : I will. Don't worry.

Caller : **Bye, then.**

Sitara : **Bye**, Arun.

DIALOGUE 5 (INFORMAL)

(The phone rings in Anil's home.)

Anil : **Hello. 27462132.**

Caller : **Hey,** Anil. **It's me, Kiran.**

Anil : **Hi,** Kiran. **Great to hear you**. Where've you been all these days?

Caller : I was at the cricket coaching camp.

Anil : Good for you. How did it go?

Caller : Great. Let's meet this evening. I'll tell you all about it.

Anil : Yes, let's. I'll meet you at the canteen.

Caller : **Right. Bye**.

Anil : **Bye.**

Useful points to remember

✎ At the beginning of a telephone conversation:
- the person who answers the call says *Hello* and gives either the phone number or a name.
- the person who calls identifies herself / himself.

✎ In the middle of the conversation:
- in formal conversations, the persons speaking on the telephone exchange information, keeping the dialogue brief and to the point.

– in informal conversations, they may talk to each other a little longer and also exchange news.

✎ To end / close the conversation:

– they may say *Bye* or *Thank you* / *Thanks* or *That's all right* / *That's okay*, depending on the context.

✎ Notice that the voice of the speakers moves from low to high:

– when they say *Hello*.

– when they make polite requests, as in
Could I talk to Mr Surendra, please.
Hold the line, please.
Could you hold the line, please.

– when they ask questions politely, as in
May I know who's calling?
Would you like to speak to her?

✎ You have learned to use shortened forms such as *I'll, I'm, we're, don't* and *can't* while speaking. But remember that at the end of a sentence:

– you cannot use shortened forms like *I'll*, *he's* and *we're*. For example:
A: Raju, will you come to the temple tomorrow?
B: Sure, *I will*. (**not** *I'll)*

– you can, however, use negative shortened forms such as *can't*, *don't* and *won't*. For example:
A: Rashmi, could you help me with my homework, please.
B: I'm sorry, Asif, I *can't*. I have a test tomorrow.

✎ While talking on the telephone, people sometimes use:

– verbless sentences, for e.g. *Nothing much*, *Great*, *Good for you*.

– incomplete sentences, for e.g. *Just wanted to make sure* (instead of *I just wanted to make sure*) and *Let's* (instead of *Let's meet this evening.)*

ACTIVITY 1

Listen carefully to the sample dialogues again and repeat each line aloud for practice.

PAIR WORK

ACTIVITY 2

Complete the telephone conversations below with suitable lines spoken by the persons answering the calls. Compare your dialogues with those that you will hear on CD and enact them with your partner.

a. *A*: ………………………………………… .
B: Could I speak to Dr Johnson, please.
A: ……………………………………………… .
B: I'm Mini Anand from Advanced Techno Solutions.
A: ………, ma'am. I'll ……………………………………… .
B: Thank you.

b. *A*: ………………………………………… .
B: Hi! Is that Sudha? Mary here. Can I speak to Lata, please.
A: ……………………………………………… .
B: Sure, I'll hold the line. Thanks.

c. *A*: ………………………………………… .
B: Hello, auntie. This is Sandeep. How're you?
A: I'm ……………, ………… . When……………………?
B: I got back yesterday. Thought I'll drop in and see you and uncle this evening.
A: That'll ……………… . ……………… this evening.
B: Okay, I'll be there by five. Bye!
A: ……………… .

ACTIVITY 3

Complete the telephone conversations below with the lines spoken by the callers. Compare your dialogues with those that you will hear on CD.

a. *A*: Hello. 24915707.
B: Hello. ………………………… .

A: Could I tell her who's calling, please.
B: .... Prasad Mohan .... MRS Steel Tubes.
A: Thank you, sir. I'll put you through to Ms Anand.
B: ....

b. *A*: Good morning. Anita John.
B: .... Dr John, ...
A: May I know who's calling, please.
B: ....
A: Hold the line, please, Ms Hasan. Dr John will speak to you in a moment.
B: ....

c. *A*: Hello. 27842710.
B: ...., Aslam. .... Vinod.
A: Hi! How're you?
B: Fine, ... Can .... Aruna, please.
A: Sure. Can you hold on? I'll call her.
B: ....

ACTIVITY 4

Work in pairs and enact the dialogues that you completed above.

ACTIVITY 5

Work in pairs. Each of you can write a short dialogue similar to the samples given. (For e.g., Chitra speaks to Mrs Vidya Mohan and asks for her daughter, Mala.) One of the situations in your dialogues could be formal, and the other informal.

ACTIVITY 6

Enact one of the two dialogues you prepare before the class.

MODULE 2

UNIT 7

DEALING WITH A WRONG NUMBER

When you answer the telephone, you sometimes find that the caller has got a wrong number. The caller has either got connected to your number by mistake or has got the telephone number wrong, which means that the person he/she wants is not available on your number. This unit will help you learn what to say in such a situation. Note that in this situation there is really no difference in the language you will use for calls made in formal and informal contexts.

फोन घेताना कधी जाणवते की फोन करणाऱ्याला चुकीचा नंबर मिळालेला आहे. त्याला/तिला चुकून तुमचा नंबर लागला आहे किंवा त्याच्याकडचा नंबर चुकीचा आहे. याचा अर्थ त्याला/तिला हवी असलेली व्यक्ती तुमच्या नंबरवर उपलब्ध नाही. अशा वेळी कसे बोलावे यासाठी या पाठात तुम्हाला मदत मिळणार आहे. लक्षात असू द्या की अशा परिस्थितीत औपचारिक किंवा अनौपचारिक दूरध्वनीमधील भाषेत फरक असणार नाही.

Listen carefully to the telephone conversations below and follow them in the book.

DIALOGUE 1

(The phone rings in Kartik's home.)

Kartik : **Hello.**
Caller : **Hello, can I speak to** Dr Narasimha, **please**?
Kartik : **Which number did you dial?** (or **Which number d'you want?**)
Caller : 52419673.
Kartik : **I'm afraid you've got the wrong number**. This is 52419672.

Caller : **Oh, I'm sorry.**
Kartik : **That's okay.**

DIALOGUE 2

(The phone rings in Dr D'Souza's clinic.)

Secretary : **Hello. Dr D'Souza's clinic.**
Caller : **Can I have** an appointment for this evening, **please**. I have bad toothache[7.2].
Secretary : **I'm sorry, ma'am. This is** Dr Susan D'Souza's number. She's a general physician, not a dentist.
Caller : **But I thought I had called** Dr D'Souza, the dentist.
Secretary : **That's** Dr Tony D'Souza. **His number is** 29897153, **ma'am.**
Caller : **I'm so sorry.**
Secretary : **That's all right.**

DIALOGUE 3

(The phone rings in Fatima's home.)

Fatima : **Hello.**
Caller : **Hello, can I speak to** Mr Sharma, **please?**
Fatima : **Sorry, but this is** Mr Ahmed's residence.
Caller : **Isn't it** 29816032?
Fatima : **No, it's** 29816033.
Caller : **Sorry to bother you.**
Fatima : **It's no bother at all.**

DIALOGUE 4

(The phone rings in Mary's home.)

Mary : **Hello,** Mr George's **residence.**
Caller : **But I called** Mr R. S. Rao's number, 2319 4378.

[7.2] Note that we do not say 'I have *a bad toothache*', but 'I have *bad toothache*'. However, we say 'I have *a bad headache*', and not 'I have *bad headache*.'

Mary : **You're right. But** Mr Rao **doesn't live here any longer**. He moved a month ago.

Caller : **I'm so sorry to have bothered you.**

Mary : **Not at all.**

Caller : **Thanks** for the information.

Mary : **You're welcome.** (or **Any time.**)

Dialogue 5

(The phone rings in Seema's home. It is her friend Sarah calling.)

Seema : **Hello.**

Caller : **Oh,** Seema! **Sorry, I thought I was calling** Rashmi.

Seema : Trust you to be absent-minded. But that's okay.

Caller : **I'll talk to you later. Bye for now.**

Seema : **Bye.**

Activity 1

Listen again to the dialogues on CD and repeat each line for practice.

PAIR WORK

Activity 2

Work in pairs. Enact each telephone conversation above with your partner.

Activity 3

Working in pairs, complete the telephone conversations below. Compare your dialogues with those that you will hear on CD and enact them with your partner.

a. *A*: Hello.

B: .... Could .... Ms Priti Raju, please.

A: I'm sorry, but there's no one here named Priti Raju.
B: .... 27115778?
A: No, this is 27115728.
B: ....
A: It's no bother at all.

b. *A*: ....
B: Good evening. May I speak to Iqbal, please.
A: ....27462829.
B: I'm sorry. I must have got the wrong number.
A: ....

GROUP WORK

ACTIVITY 4

Form two groups. One group can be the *Callers*, and the other can be the *Responders*. A person from the caller group can call a wrong number, and someone from the responder group can deal with it. You can use the words in bold from the sample dialogues to enact the situations.

ACTIVITY 5 →

Working in pairs, think of a situation dealing with a wrong number and write a short dialogue. After you finish, enact the dialogue before your group.

MODULE 2

UNIT 8

TAKING AND LEAVING MESSAGES

Sometimes, when we answer a phone call or make one, the person who is needed is either not available or is busy and cannot take the call at that time. In such a situation, the caller can leave a message. This unit will help you learn how to take and leave telephone messages. The sample dialogues below are set in formal as well as informal contexts.

फोन करताना किंवा घेताना कधी हवी असलेली व्यक्ती एकतर उपलब्ध नसते किंवा कामात असते आणि त्यावेळी फोन घेऊ शकत नाही. अशा परिस्थितीत फोन करणारी व्यक्ती निरोप देऊन ठेऊ शकते. दूरध्वनीवर निरोप कसे घ्यावे किंवा द्यावे याविषयी तुम्हाला या पाठात मदत मिळणार आहे. औपचारिक तसेच अनौपचारिक संदर्भातील नमुना संभाषणे खाली दिली आहेत.

DIALOGUE 1 (FORMAL)

(The phone rings in Mr Ansari's home.)

Mrs Ansari : **Hello.**

Caller : **Hello,** I'm Jeevan Prasad. **Could I speak to** Mr Ansari, **please.**

Mrs Ansari : He's gone out. **Can I take a message?**

Caller : **Yes. Please tell** Mr Ansari **I called. And could you ask him to call me back at** 48723434, **please**. It's urgent.

Mrs Ansari : **Could you repeat the number please,** Mr Prasad.

Caller : 48 – 72 – 34 – 34. **Have you got that now?**

Mrs Ansari : Yes. 48 – 72 – 34 – 34. **I'll tell** Mr Ansari **that you called.**

Caller : **Thank you.**

Mrs Ansari : **You're welcome.**

DIALOGUE 2 (FORMAL)

(The phone rings in the Medak Girls Government Junior College.)

Secretary : **Good morning.** Girls Government Junior College, Medak.

Caller : **Good morning. Could I speak to** Professor Raman, **please.**

Secretary : Professor Raman is on leave. **May I know who's calling?**

Caller : **I'm** Jabbar Ali, from Mehbubia College. **Could I leave a message, please.**

Secretary : **Just a minute, sir.** *(pause)* **Yes?**

Caller : **Please tell** him that the meeting to be held on 15th April has been postponed to 4th May.

Secretary : **D'you mind repeating that, sir?**

Caller : The meeting scheduled for 15th April has been postponed to 4th May.

Secretary : **Anything else, sir?**

Caller : **You can ask him to call me** if he needs any more information. **My number is** 28453536.

Secretary : 28453536. **I certainly will**, Dr Ali.

Caller : **Thank you.**

Secretary : **You're welcome**, sir.

DIALOGUE 3 (FORMAL)

(The phone rings in the CSI Hospital.)

Secretary : **Hello. Good afternoon.** CSI Hospital.

Caller : **Good afternoon, I'd like to speak to** Dr Nandita Desai, **please.**

Secretary : **Dr Desai's** in the operation theatre, sir. **I can take a message.**
Caller : **Thank you. Could you tell her** Rajesh Rao **called, please.**
Secretary : **I'll do that**, sir. **Would you like to leave your phone number?**
Caller : **Dr Desai has my number. Thank you.**
Secretary : **You're welcome.**

DIALOGUE 4 (INFORMAL)

(The phone rings in Bharat's home.)

Bharat : **Hello.**
Caller : **Hello. I'm** Rani. **Is** Rekha **there?**
Bharat : **Hi,** Rani. **I'm** Bharat, Rekha's brother. She's gone to the music class. **I'll tell her you called**.
Caller : **Thanks**, Bharat. **Please tell her I'll talk to her in the evening**.
Bharat : **Okay.**
Caller : **Thanks. Bye**.
Bharat : **Bye.**

DIALOGUE 5 (INFORMAL)

(The phone rings in Vasu's home.)

Vasu : **Hello.**
Caller : **Hello.** Suresh mama? Priya **here.**
Vasu : **Hi,** Priya. **This is** Vasu. Father's gone to the market. **Anything important?**
Caller : **No, not really. Just tell him that** I've got the book he wanted. I'll bring it when I come on Sunday.
Vasu : **Right. I'll tell** him **that.**
Caller : **Thanks,** Vasu. And how're your exams going?
Vasu : All right. I have the last one tomorrow.
Caller : Good luck. I'll see you on Sunday then.
Vasu : Yes. **Bye.**
Caller : **Bye, bye.**

Useful points to remember

During informal phone calls:

✎ We do not usually use fixed expressions of politeness, such as
- *Can I speak to Rekha, please.*
- *May I know who's calling / speaking?*
- *Would you like to leave a message?*
- *Would you like me to take a message?*
- *Could I leave a message, please.*

✎ We often use the name of the person we are talking to, to sound friendly:
- *Hi, Rani.*
- *Thanks, Bharat.*

ACTIVITY 1

Listen again to the telephone conversations carefully and repeat each line aloud for practice.

PAIR WORK

ACTIVITY 2

Work in pairs. Enact the sample dialogues above twice, so that each of you plays the roles of the persons making the calls and taking them.

ACTIVITY 3

Working in pairs, complete the telephone conversations below. Compare your dialogues with those that you will hear on CD and enact the dialogues with your partner.

a. *A*: Hello. Panchayat office.
   B: ...., Mr Joseph, please.
   A: Mr Joseph is in a meeting. Could I take a message, please.
   B: .... Salman Baig .... Agro Services. .... at 24271563, ...

A: Yes, I'll give him your message, Mr Baig.
B: ....

b. *A*: ....
B: Good morning. I'd like to speak to Shanti, please.
A: .... college. .... speaking, please.
B: I'm Sameer Choudhury, a colleague. Could I leave a message, please.
A: ....
B: Please tell Shanti (that) I have the book she wanted, and (that) I'll give it to her in college tomorrow. My number is 26827102.
A: .... Is that right?
B: Yes, thank you.
A: ....

c. *A*: .... 27340156.
B: ...., Mani. Shobha here. Can I speak to auntie?
A: ...., Shobha. Mother's resting. She has a terrible headache. Is there anything .... to tell her?
B: Yes. I wanted the recipe for the tomato chutney she sent us yesterday. .... (that) I'll call again in the evening, ...
A: .... tell her.
B: ....
A: You're welcome, Shobha.

GROUP WORK

ACTIVITY 4

Form groups of ten. Each group can imagine two situations, one formal and the other informal. For e.g., the members of group 1 can imagine that they are attending a science conference. One of them can be the secretary, and the others can be the participants. The participants can try to contact one another on telephone through the secretary. They can leave messages, and he/she can take messages. Similarly, think of an informal situation. Write short dialogues and enact them. Use the expressions in bold. You can also correct one another.

Module 2

Unit 9 Making Inquiries on the Phone

You often need to use the telephone to get some information or make an inquiry to find out, for example, the time of arrival of a train or the last date for the sale of application forms or whether classes will be held on a particular day. In doing this, you have to be clear, brief and polite. This will make it easy for you to get the information you want. The unit will help you learn how to use English to make inquiries.

माहिती घेण्यासाठी किंवा चौकशी करण्यासाठी तुम्हाला बऱ्याच वेळा फोन करावे लागतात; उदा. एखाद्या रेल्वेगाडीची येण्याची वेळ, नमुना अर्जांच्या विक्रीची शेवटची तारीख, एखाद्या विशिष्ट दिवशी वर्ग असणार आहे की नाही. हे करताना तुम्ही सुस्पष्ट, थोडक्यात व सभ्यपणे बोलायला हवे. यामुळे माहिती मिळणे सोपे होईल. अशी चौकशी करताना इंग्लिशचा वापर कसा करावा हे शिकण्यासाठी या पाठात तुम्हाला मदत मिळेल.

Listen to the dialogues below and follow them in your book.

Dialogue 1 

(The phone rings in a railway inquiry office.)

Railway inquiry : **Good afternoon**. Railway inquiry.

Caller : **Could you tell me when the** Rajdhani Express **to** Delhi **leaves, please.**

Railway inquiry : **At 7.10 in the morning, ma'am.**

Caller : **Is it a daily train?**

Railway inquiry : **No, ma'am. It runs** five **days a week**. Monday to Friday.

Caller : **Thank you very much.**

Railway inquiry : **My pleasure, ma'am.**

DIALOGUE 2

(The phone rings in the office of Yatri Nivas.The receptionist takes the call.)

Receptionist : **Good morning.** Yatri Nivas.

Caller : **What time does** the Volvo coach **leave for** Shirdi, **please**?

Receptionist : **There are** two coaches **to** Shirdi **every** Friday. **One at** 16 hundred hours **and the other at** 18 hundred hours[9.2].

Caller : **Could you reserve** ten seats **on the 6 p.m. coach, please.**

Receptionist : **In whose name should I make the booking, sir?**

Caller : **It's for** Lakshman Reddy and family.

Receptionist : **Yes, sir. I'll repeat that.** Ten **seats for** Mr Lakshman Reddy and family **on the** 6 o'clock Volvo.

Caller : **That's right. Thank you.**

Receptionist : **You're welcome, sir.**

DIALOGUE 3

(The phone rings in the APSRTC inquiry office.)

APSRTC inquiry : **Hello.** APSRTC inquiry.

Caller : **Good morning. Could you tell me what the fare to** Vijayawada **would be, please. I'd like to travel by the** 12 noon Express.

APSRTC inquiry : **It's** Rs 400.

Caller : **Pardon? Could you repeat that, please.**

APSRTC : **The fare is** rupees four hundred.

9.2 Note that the 12-hour system of expressing time uses the numerals 1–12 followed by *a.m.* (from midnight until before noon) and *p.m.* (from noon until before midnight). Thus, 12 a.m. represents midnight, and 12 p.m. noon. Under the 24-hour system of expressing time, usually used by people, for e.g., in the travel and tourism industries, the hours are numbered from 0000 hours (spoken as zero zero zero zero hours) for midnight to 2359 hours (spoken as twenty-three fifty-nine hours) for 11.59 p.m.

Caller : **Thank you very much.**
APSRTC : **You're welcome**, ma'am.

DIALOGUE 4

(The phone rings in the Government Science College.)

Office assistant : **Hello.** GSC.
Caller : **Good afternoon. Could you tell me when you'll begin issuing application forms for** the BA first year course, **please.**
Office assistant : **From** Thursday, 20th April.
Caller : **What would be the price of** a form?
Office assistant : Fifty rupees, ma'am.
Caller : **What're your timings for the sale of the forms, please?**
Office assistant : Ten **to** four **every day, from** Monday **to** Friday.
Caller : **I would also like to know the last date for the issue of the forms, please.**
Office assistant : 12th May, ma'am.
Caller : **Thank you.**
Office assistant : **Most welcome**, ma'am.

ACTIVITY 1

Listen to the dialogues above again and repeat the lines spoken by the person making inquiries.

PAIR WORK

ACTIVITY 2

Enact the dialogues with a partner. Take turns so that each of you gets a chance to play the roles of the person answering the call and the person making inquiries.

Note that inquiries over the phone are usually similar to those that we make directly at an inquiry office or across a counter. Look at some questions that can be used to make inquiries.

Purpose	Expression
1. Asking for the time of departure/ arrival of train/plane/bus	a. Could you tell me when …, please. b. Could you let me know when . . ., please. c. What time does …,please? d. When does ………., please?
2. Asking for frequency	a. Is it a daily/ biweekly /weekly …..? b. How often does ……….?
3. Asking for the fare	a. What would be the fare to ………, please? b. Can you tell me the fare to ……., please. c. Could you tell me how much a ticket to … costs, please.
4. Asking for a booking	a. Can you book …….., please. b. Can you reserve …….., please. c. Could you book me on ……, please. d. I'd like to book ………, please.
5. Asking about the issue of forms	a. Could you tell me when you will issue forms for….., please. b. What would be the price of a form, please? c. When will forms for …… be available, please? d. When will you begin issuing forms, please?

ACTIVITY 3

Working in pairs, complete the telephone conversations below using some of the expressions given above. Compare your dialogues with those that you will hear on CD and enact them with your partner.

a. *A*: Hello. Vizag Shipping Company.
B: Good evening. I'd like to know if .... send cargo through you to Chennai, ...
A: Yes, we do carry cargo to Chennai and Mumbai.
B: .... a week do you offer the service, ...?
A: We have a cargo service twice a week, on Mondays and Thursdays.
B: ....
A: You're wecome.

b. *A*: Hello. Railway inquiries.
B: .... the Bangalore Express leaves Kachiguda station, ...
A: At 7.15 in the evening, sir.
B: ....
A: You're welcome.

c. *A*: Good morning. Railway inquiries.
B: .... How many .... the Falaknuma Express go to Kolkata, ...?
A: Daily, ma'am.
B: ....
A: You're welcome, ma'am.

d. *A*: Hello. Mercury Travels.
B: I'd .... four seats on the Deluxe bus to Srikakulam, ...
A: Could you give me the date of journey, please.
B: ....
A: It'll be done, sir. You could pick up the tickets tomorrow evening.
B: ....
A: Glad to be of service, sir.

e. *A*: Hello. APSRTC inquiries.
   B: Good afternoon. Could............from Kakinada to Warangal, ...
   A: It's Rs 550 for the non-A/C coach.
   B: ....much.
   A: You're welcome, ma'am.

GROUP WORK

ACTIVITY 4

1. Form groups of ten.
2. On sheets of paper, write down five dialogues for different situations where inquiries are made on the telephone.
3. Fold the sheets of paper and jumble them up.
4. Now choose a partner and pick up one of the folded sheets.
5. Each pair can practise its dialogue and then enact it before the group.

MODULE 2

UNIT 10 — CALLING FOR HELP IN AN EMERGENCY

One of the times when we need to use the telephone is in case of an emergency—to ask for urgent help. Thus, we may have to ask for an ambulance or call the police, a fire station or a flood relief centre. This unit will help you learn what to say when you call a helpline.

> आणीबाणीच्या वेळी ताबडतोबीने मदत मिळावी म्हणून एखादवेळी फोन करण्याची वेळ येते, जसे रुग्णवाहिका हवी म्हणून, पोलीसांना किंवा अग्निशमन दलाला बोलावण्यासाठी किंवा पूरग्रस्तांना मदत करणाऱ्या केन्द्राकडे विचारणा करण्यासाठी. मदतीसाठी विचारणा करताना काय बोलावे हे शिकताना तुम्हाला या पाठात मदत मिळेल.

Listen to the dialogue below on CD and follow it in the book.

DIALOGUE 1 (CALLING FOR AN AMBULANCE)

(The phone rings at 108.)

Ambulance service : **Hello, ambulance service.**

Caller : **I'm** Rajesh Kumar **calling from** a public booth. **There's been an accident at** the crossroads **near** Sangeet cinema **in** Secunderabad. A motorcyclist is hurt badly. He's bleeding.

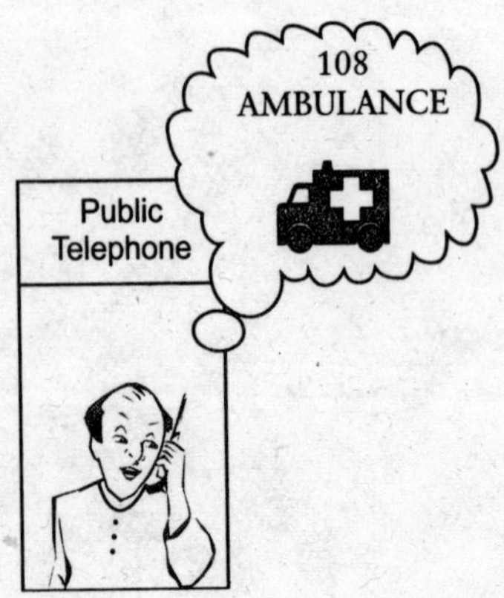

Ambulance service : **Don't move him. Just make him comfortable. We'll be there soon.**

Caller : **Thank you.**

DIALOGUE 2 (CALLING FOR A FIRE ENGINE)

(The phone rings at 101.)

Fire service : **Hello. Fire station.**

Caller : **My names's** Ramani Devraj. **A fire has broken out at** the Ansari Shopping Complex, Mall Road. **Please send the fire engines soon.**

Fire service : **They're** already **on their way**, ma'am. **They should be there anytime now.**

Caller : **Thank you.**

DIALOGUE 3 (CALLING THE POLICE)

(The phone rings at 100.)

Police helpline : **Hello, police helpline.**

Caller : **There's been a burglary** next door. The door is broken. The owners are out of town.

Helpline : **Your name, please?**

Caller : Srinivasulu Naidu.

Helpline : **Address and phone number?**

Caller : **It's** 121 – 10 – 36, Kakatiya Nagar, Secunderabad. **The house is behind** the St John's church. **My phone number is** 2714 5306.

Helpline : **I'll repeat that**, sir. **Address** 121 – 10 – 36, Kakatiya Nagar, Secunderabad, **behind** St John's church. **Phone** 2714 5306.

Caller : **That's right.**

Helpline : **Please don't touch anything. We'll be there in five minutes.**

Caller : **Thank you.**

DIALOGUE 4: (CALLING THE SENIOR CITIZENS HELPLINE)

(The phone rings at 1090.)

S.C. helpline : **Hello, senior citizens helpline. Can I help you, please.** (or **May I help you, please.**)

Caller : **Yes, please. I'm** Ameena Husain. My grandmother has fallen from her bed, and I'm alone in the house with her.

Helpline : **Don't worry. We'll be with you in a minute.**

Caller : **Thank you.**

Helpline : **Your address, please?**

Caller : **16 – 3 – 740 Fateh Sultan Lane.**

Helpline : **Sorry? What was that?**

Caller : **Fateh Sultan Lane. F-A-T-E-H S-U-L-T-A-N Lane. It's in** Nampally.

Helpline : **I've got it, thanks.** Relax and wait for us. **Bye.**

Useful points to remember

- People you are talking to may use incomplete question forms when you are in a hurry. For e.g.,
  - *Your name, please?* instead of *What's your name?*
  - *Address and phone number?* instead of *What's your name and phone number?*
- When you call someone in an emergency, you have to say your name, address and phone number slowly and clearly.
- Sometimes you may have to spell out certain words, for example *F–A–T–E–H S–U–L–T–A–N*, because the person at the other end of the line may not have heard it correctly. You may also need to make a letter in a word clear by giving another word in which it appears, for e.g. *'F' as in 'fish'*.
- Note that when the speakers in the dialogues want to say something slowly and clearly or they want to draw attention to some words, they say it with extra force, for e.g. *Hundred and twenty one dash ten dash thirty six Kakatiya Nagar* and *I'm alone in the house with her.*

Activity 1

Listen to the dialogues again and repeat the lines spoken by the caller.

PAIR WORK

Activity 2

Work in pairs. Enact the above dialogues, taking turns to play the roles of the caller and the helpline service.

GROUP WORK

Activity 3

Form groups of five and write two short dialogues of four to five lines for situations in which someone has to call an emergency service. Each group will enact one dialogue before the class. Here are a few samples you could use.

a. Leena finds smoke coming out of her neighbour's locked flat. She calls the fire station and asks for help, giving her address and telephone number clearly.
b. Venkat sees a man being robbed. He calls the police and reports the crime, giving the exact location.
c. A lorry has dashed against a scooter. The rider is badly hurt. A passerby calls an ambulance and gives his / her name and the exact location.
d. An elderly person in the family complains of a severe pain in the chest. Joseph calls an emergency service.

Here are some expressions you can use to seek help on telephone in case of an emergency.

1. there's been
2. there's a
3. someone's
4. an unruly mob

5. a broken leg
6. lying unconscious
7. has caught fire
8. has swallowed a pin
9. breaking streetlights and damaging buses
10. the water's rising fast
11. has/have fallen into a well
12. roof / walls has/have collapsed
13. has/have fallen into an open drain
14. attacked and robbed
15. trapped inside a building on fire
16. has /have been swept away by the water
17. transformer's not working
18. gas cylinder's leaking
19. send someone immediately
20. missing from home since

MODULE 3

UNIT 11

GETTING PEOPLE'S ATTENTION AND INTERRUPTING

It sometimes happens that we have to politely get people's attention before we can speak to them. Also, sometimes when we need to speak urgently to a person who is busy doing something or talking to someone else, we have to interrupt—again, politely. These are important skills that every speaker of English will need to learn and practise, and this unit will help you do so.

कधी लोकांशी बोलण्याआधी नम्रपणे त्यांचे लक्ष वेधून घ्यावे लागते.त्याचप्रमाणे कधी एखादी व्यक्ती दुसऱ्या कोणाशी तरी बोलण्यात किंवा कामात व्यग्र असते, अशा वेळी अत्यंत तातडीचे काम असल्यास आपल्याला त्या व्यक्तीशी मध्येच बोलावे लागते - अर्थात नम्रपणे. इंग्लिशमध्ये बोलणाऱ्या प्रत्येक व्यक्तीला ही कौशल्ये आत्मसात करावी लागतील, त्यांचा सराव करावा लागेल. या पाठात याबाबत मदत मिळू शकेल.

Listen carefully to the following dialogues on CD and follow them in the book.

DIALOGUE 1 (FORMAL)

(Jayaram wants to get the attention of his science teacher, who is in the staff room correcting examination scripts.)

Jayaram : **Excuse me, ma'am. I know (that) you're busy, but may I speak to you for a moment?**

Teacher : Yes, Jayaram? **What can I do for you?**

Jayaram : It's about the chart for the science exhibition. Can I make one with pictures of what a healthy diet should include?

Teacher : I think that's a good idea, Jayaram. The chart will look attractive with pictures.

Jayaram : Thank you, ma'am. **Sorry to have bothered you.**

Teacher : **That's all right**, Jayaram.

DIALOGUE 2 (FORMAL)

(Manjula needs to give the principal, who is in a staff meeting, a message. She stands at the door of the staff room to get his attention.)

Principal (*noticing Manjula at the door*) : Yes, Manjula, what is it?

Manjula : Sir, **sorry to interrupt, but** someone's come to see you. He's from the Board of Intermediate Education.

Principal : Thank you, Manjula. Please tell him I'll be coming in a minute. He could wait in my office.

Manjula : Yes, sir.

DIALOGUE 3 (FORMAL)

(Roopa interrupts two strangers talking to each other at a bus stop.)

Roopa : **Pardon me, but** could you tell me which bus goes to the railway station from here?

Stranger : 47 B.

Roopa : Thanks. **I'm sorry I interrupted your conversation.**

Stranger : **That's okay.**

DIALOGUE 4 (INFORMAL)

(Veena is among her friends. Something occurs to her suddenly and she butts into the conversation to ask a question.)

Veena : **Just a minute.** Does anyone know if Mrs Sharma is leaving for Allahabad tomorrow?

Naresh : I think she is.

Veena : Thanks. I need to send a packet for Sunder with her. **Sorry, what were we talking about?** Oh, yes, the movie . . .

DIALOGUE 5 (INFORMAL)

(Suresh walks up to his friends who are chatting over coffee in the canteen.)

Suresh : **Sorry, am I interrupting?** I came to ask if some of you could come to college on Sunday. We need people to help us decorate the place for the Independence Day celebrations.

Tony : **Sure**, we can come. What time?

Suresh : About ten, let's say. **I think you were in the middle of something. Sorry I disturbed you.**

Leena : **It was nothing important.** Come and join us for coffee.

Suresh : Thanks. I'd love to.

Useful points to remember

- When trying to get someone's attention, it is polite to wait until the person looks at you.
- One way of getting someone's attention or interrupting someone to say something to them without causing offence is to begin with an apology (*Sorry / Sorry to bother you /Excuse me)* followed by *but* and your reason for wanting to speak to the person. Your tone should indicate that you feel sorry about interrupting.
- When someone tries to get your attention or interrupts when you are busy or engaged in conversation with others, it is polite to respond with words that sound friendly and encouraging (for example, *That's all right / No problem /Sure*).

Here are some other expressions you can use to interrupt or get someone's attention and to respond when someone else does so.

Pardon me . . .	Yes?
Pardon the interruption, but . . .	That's all right.
I hate to interrupt you, but . . .	No problem.
I don't want to interrupt you, but . . .	Sure.

(contd...)

I'm sorry to interrupt you, but . . .	Not at all.
Could I interrupt . . .?	Yes? What can I do for you?
Excuse me, but d'you have a moment?	Of course.
I'm sorry, but . . .	It's not a bother.
Are you free for a minute?	
Have you got a minute?	
Could I just ask . . .?	
Excuse me, but . . .	
Sorry to butt in, but . . .	
Sorry, but could I ask you a quick question?	

ACTIVITY 1

Listen to the sample dialogues again and repeat each line for practice.

PAIR WORK

ACTIVITY 2

Enact dialogues 1–5 with your partner, taking turns to play the role of the person trying to get someone's attention / interrupting as well as that of the person responding to the interruption.

ACTIVITY 3

Complete the following dialogues with suitable expressions that you have learnt in the unit. After you finish, compare your dialogues with those you will hear on CD and enact them with your partner.

a. (Pratap goes to the staff room to get the world map. He sees two teachers talking to each other.)

Pratap : ...., but could I take the world map, please?
Teacher : Sure, Pratap. D'you have a geography class now?
Pratap : Yes, ma'am. I'm ....
Teacher : That's all right, Pratap.

b. (*Sujata meets her friends in the park and tells them that her sister's getting married.)*

Sujata : ....

Vivek : Don't worry, Sujata. We were only talking about the weather. But you look excited. What's the news?

Sujata : My sister's wedding is fixed! She's getting married this summer.

Salim : How wonderful! Sit down. Tell us more.

Sujata : I can't. I've got to go home. The groom's people are coming for dinner. I must help my mother. ....

Vivek : .... You've brought us great news.

c. (*Joshi walks up to his boss and tries to get his attention.)*

Joshi : ...., sir. .... a minute?

Boss : .... Come in, Joshi.

Joshi : ...., sir.

GROUP WORK

ACTIVITY 4

Form groups of four or five. Every member of the group can take turns to interrupt the others and get their attention, and each of the others in the group can respond suitably. Use the additional expressions in the list above as well as the words in bold in the sample dialogues, making sure that none of the expressions is repeated.

MODULE 3

UNIT 12 GIVING INSTRUCTIONS AND SEEKING CLARIFICATIONS

This unit deals with the language you will use in order to give instructions clearly. The unit will also tell you how to ask someone to make clear something that they said and that you did not understand, or to repeat themselves if you did not hear them clearly the first time. The language you use to do this must be polite or else you are likely to offend the person.

सूचना स्पष्टपणे देण्यासाठी भाषा कशी वापरावी याविषयी या पाठात सांगितले आहे. दुसऱ्या कोणी आपल्याला काही सांगितलेले आपल्याला कळले नसेल तर ते परत स्पष्टपणे सांगावे यासाठी किंवा त्यांचे बोलणे स्पष्ट ऐकू आले नसल्यास त्याची पुनरावृत्ती करण्यासाठी, समोरच्या व्यक्तीला कसे सांगावे हेही या पाठात सांगितले आहे. हे करताना भाषा अत्यंत अदबीने वापरली पाहिजे, नाहीतर तुमच्याकडून त्या व्यक्तीचा अपमान होऊ शकेल.

To learn how to give instructions, listen carefully to the dialogues below on CD and follow them in the book.

DIALOGUE 1

(An art teacher tells his students how to make a kite.)

Teacher : **Let's learn to make** a kite today. **We'll need** a plastic bag, two sticks, a reel of cord, scotch tape and a pair of scissors.

Satish : **Excuse me**, sir. **What's** cord, **please**?

Teacher : It's the thick thread we use to fly kites, Satish. Okay? Then, shall we continue? Now, **follow my instructions carefully**.

First, **cut** a square sheet out of the plastic bag. **Then**, **make** a large round hole in the centre of the sheet. **Next**, **make** a cross with the two sticks and tie them together tightly with the cord. **Now**, **tie** four pieces of cord of the same length to each corner of the frame **and**, **attach** the plastic sheet firmly to the frame with scotch tape. **Then tie** the loose ends of the pieces of cord together to the reel. **Add** two tails to the bottom of the kite for balance. **Now**, the kite is ready. **Is that clear to everyone?**

Students : Yes, sir. Thank you.

DIALOGUE 2

(Renu instructs her brother, Jeevan, on how to make tea.)

Jeevan : Renu, can you teach me to make tea?

Renu : Don't worry. **I'll teach you step by step. You can't go wrong.** Let's begin. **Step 1, put** one and a half cups of water into a small pan.

Jeevan : That will make two cups of tea, won't it?

Renu : Right—it will, when you add the milk. **Now, step 2, light** the stove **and place** the vessel on it. When the water begins to boil, **add** a teaspoonful of tea leaves to it **and let it** simmer for a minute.

Jeevan : Will one teaspoonful of tea leaves do?

Renu : Yes, the tea will become too strong and bitter if we add more. **Next, step 3. Strain** the tea **and add** half a cup of milk, and sugar to taste. One spoon per cup should do unless you want it sweeter. **Now, the** tea**'s ready.**

Jeevan : Hey, that's simple. Thanks, Renu.

Renu : Anytime, Jeevan.

DIALOGUE 3

(A mathematics teacher gives his students instructions on how to draw a figure.)

Teacher : Follow my instructions carefully and draw the diagram. **First, start with** a point somewhere in the middle of the page. **Second,** with the help of a scale / ruler, **mark off** 5 centimetres on either side of the point **and draw** a horizontal line.

Mala : Sir, **do we** draw a horizontal line measuring 10 centimetres through the point?

Teacher : Exactly. You've got it right, Mala. (*to the class*) **Now, for the third step. Mark off** 5 centimetres vertically on either side of the point **and draw** a vertical line measuring 10 centimetres. Did you understand?

Students : Yes, sir.

Teacher : Good. **Finally, draw** four lines joining the ends of the two lines and touching each other at the corners. Can you describe the diagram you've drawn?

Raju : It's a square, sir.

Teacher : You're right, Raju.

Useful points to remember

When giving instructions, use:

- short, clear sentences
- connecting words to show the order in which the instructions have to be followed, for example *first / firstly, second/secondly, then, next, lastly…*
- imperative sentences such as *Cut a square, Make a cross, Tie the loose ends…*, each beginning with a verb in the form it appears in a dictionary (for e.g. *cut, make, tie, attach*).

ACTIVITY 1

Listen to dialogues 1–3 again and repeat each line for practice.

PAIR WORK

ACTIVITY 2

Enact the sample dialogues with your partner, taking turns to play the role of the person giving instructions.

ACTIVITY 3

Here is an incomplete set of instructions on how to make a whistle. Fill in the blanks with any one of the connecting words used in the sample dialogues. After you finish, compare your instructions with what you will hear on CD and repeat each line for practice.

a. ...., take a rectangular sheet of paper.
b. ...., fold it in half.
c. ...., fold the edge of each half backwards to meet at the middle fold.
d. The folds will look like the pleats of a sari.
e. ...., cut out a hole in the middle fold.
f. .... hold the pleated paper firmly to your mouth and blow hard to make the sound of a whistle.

ACTIVITY 4

Two sets of pictures showing the steps in making fried egg and cold coffee are given below. First, write a set of instructions for one picture each. Then, to check if your instructions are clear, listen to them on CD. Finally, you and your partner can give each other instructions on how to make the item of your choice.

① ② ③ ④

Listen carefully to the dialogues below, where people ask for clarifications, on CD and follow them in the book.

DIALOGUE 4 (FORMAL)

(Meena is in a mathematics class. She does not understand an explanation and asks the teacher for a clearer explanation.)

Meena : **Excuse me,** sir. **I'm sorry, but I didn't really understand** the definition of a subset.

Teacher : **Right. Let me explain it again.** If every element in set A is also an element of set B, then A is called a subset of B. **Have I made that clear now?**

Meena : **Yes**, sir. **Thank you**.

DIALOGUE 5 (FORMAL)

(Mary is in an office meeting. She is not clear about a point in the discussion and asks the person speaking for clarification.)

Mary : **Sorry to interrupt,** Mr Chandran, **but I'm not quite clear about** the new arrangement.

Chandran : **That's all right. I'll go through it again.** Mr Sen will look after branch office accounts and Ms Bhat will report to him. **I hope that's clear now.**

Mary : **Yes, it is. Thank you.**

DIALOGUE 6 (FORMAL)

(Roy is at a construction site. His chief engineer speaks to him, but he is not able to hear him clearly. Roy asks his senior colleague to repeat what he said.)

Roy : **Pardon? I didn't get what you said. Would you mind repeating it, sir?**

Chief engineer : **Not at all. What I said was that** the project has to be completed by August at the very latest. Our clients want to move in by September.

Roy : **Thank you,** sir.

DIALOGUE 7 (INFORMAL)

(Madhu asks his mother to clarify something she said about a relative.)

Madhu : Amma, **I didn't get what you said about** our being related to Mohan uncle.

Mother : **Okay, I'll say it again.** Mohan uncle's grandfather is your father's aunt's son. **Understood?**

Madhu : **I think so, thanks. Let me see if I have got it.** Mohan uncle's grandfather and Nana are cousins. **Right?**

Mother : **Right.**

DIALOGUE 8 (INFORMAL)

(Nandu asks his uncle to repeat his travel programme as he did not get it clear the first time.)

Nandu : Uncle, **I didn't quite catch the dates**. **Could you repeat your programme**, please.

Uncle : **Sure.** I'm leaving for Kanpur on Thursday. I'll be there until Friday. Then I'll go to Jabalpur for a week and will return to Chennai on 15th June. **Got that?**

Nandu : **Yes, I have. Thanks.**

DIALOGUE 9 (INFORMAL)

(Savita's father gives her a telephone number. She does not get it right and requests him to repeat the number.)

Father : Savita, you must call your aunt Gita when you go to Tenali tomorrow. Her mobile number is 9882754961.

Savita : **Sorry, I think I missed a digit. Could you say the number again, please.**

Father : 98-82-75-49-61. **Okay?**

Savita : **I've got it. Thanks.**

Useful points to remember

- One way of seeking a clarification is by saying that you do not understand something, which will make the other person offer to explain it again or in a different way (for e.g. *I'm not quite clear . . . / I didn't really understand . . .*). You can also ask directly for a clarification, example or explanation (for e.g. *Could you clarify . . . / Could you explain . . ./ Could you tell me how . . .*). A third way of clarifying something is to ask specific questions (for e.g. *When does. . . / How is . . . / What is the . . ./ Where can . . .*).
- When telling someone that you missed what they said or that you did not understand it, it is polite to begin with the words *Sorry* or *I'm sorry* and end with *Thanks* or *Thank you,* because you are actually making a request when you ask for clarification or repetition.
- When someone asks you to repeat what you said or give a clearer explanation, it helps the person feel that he / she has not offended you or caused you bother if you start with expressions such as *Right / Okay / Sure/ No problem/ Certainly / Of course.*

✎ After repeating or clarifying something you said on request, you can make sure that the person who asked for repetition or clarification is satisfied by asking *Is that better? / Clear? / Have you got that now? / Right?*

ACTIVITY 5

Listen to dialogues 4–9 again and repeat each line for practice.

PAIR WORK

ACTIVITY 6

Enact the sample dialogues with your partner.

ACTIVITY 7

Complete the short exchanges below, using the cues given in brackets. After you finish, compare your exchanges with what you will hear on CD and enact them with your partner.

a. *A*: Rice grows best in warm places where there is also plenty of rainfall. East Godavari district in Andhra Pradesh is an example.

B: .... (*Ask the speaker for another example of a rice-growing region.*)

A: .... Kerala is one.

B: ....

b. *A*: In science, the terms mass and weight do not mean the same thing.

B: ...., but .... (*Say you don't understand.*)

A: Okay. Let me explain it a little more. The mass of an object is the amount of matter it contains, and it remains constant. The weight of an object is the downward pulling force on it, and this changes because gravity is not constant at all places. I .... (*Check if your explanation is clear.*)

B: ...., ...

c. *A:* Revati, Prema called to say that she will be arriving by the Tirupati Express at 7 p.m. on Saturday.

B: ....
...... (Ask the speaker to repeat what she said.)

A: .... Prema's coming by the Tirupati Express at 7 p.m. on Saturday.
.... ?

B: ....

MODULE 3

UNIT 13

MAKING REQUESTS AND RESPONDING TO REQUESTS

We sometimes need to ask other people for something—help, information, directions, money or a book—and also respond when someone makes similar requests to us. It is important to know how to use language carefully to do this if you want a positive response to your request. It is also necessary to agree to a request pleasantly, without making the other person feel that the request is bothering you or that you are doing him/her a favour. In case you have to decline the request, it has to be done tactfully, without causing offence. In this unit, you will learn how to make and respond to requests politely in English.

कधीकधी आपल्याला समोरच्या व्यक्तीला काही विचारायचे असते - मदत, माहिती, पत्ता किंवा कसे जायचे, पैसे किंवा पुस्तक हवे असणे - दुसऱ्याकोणी केलेल्या अशाच विनंतीला उत्तरही द्यावयाचे असते. आपल्या विनंतीला विधायक प्रतिसाद मिळावा असे वाटत असेल तर भाषेचा वापर काळजीपूर्वक कसा करावा हे माहीत असणे महत्त्वाचे आहे. आपल्याकडे आलेली विनंती आनंदाने मान्य करणेही तेवढेच गरजेचे आहे, केलेल्या विनंतीने तुम्हाला त्रास होतो आहे किंवा ही विनंती मान्य करून तुम्ही समोरच्यावर उपकार करत आहात असे तिला वाटता कामा नये. विनंती नाकारण्याची वेळ आली तर ते अत्यंत कुशलतेने करता आले पाहिजे, ते अपमानास्पद होता कामा नये. इंग्लिशमध्ये सभ्य रीतीने विनंती कशी करावी आणि विनंतीला उत्तर कसे द्यावे हे या पाठात तुम्ही शिकणार आहात.

Listen carefully to the dialogues below on CD and follow them in the book. They are requests made in formal contexts where a person is either talking to someone he/she does not know well or to someone who is senior in position. The samples will also show you how you can agree to requests or decline them politely.

DIALOGUE 1

(Asif Abbas goes to his general manager, Mr Jain, with a request for a month's leave.)

Asif : Good morning, Mr Jain.

Mr Jain : Good morning, Abbas. What's the matter? You look worried.

Asif : My son is unwell and needs to have an operation. **I'd be grateful if you could permit me to** take ten days leave.

Mr Jain : **That shouldn't be a problem.** Das can take care of your projects while you are away.

Asif : **Thank you very much,** Mr Jain.

Mr Jain : **You're welcome,** Abbas. Don't worry. Your son's going to be fine.

DIALOGUE 2

(Mrs Vasudev speaks to a person at a bank and asks him how to open a bank account.)

Mrs Vasudev : Excuse me, **could you help me, please.**

Bank official : Yes, ma'am? **What can I do for you?**

Mrs Vasudev : **I'd like to** open an account in your bank. **Could you tell me how I can** do it, **please.**

Bank official : **Certainly**, ma'am. **I'd be happy to.** Please be seated. I'll explain.

Mrs Vasudev : **Thank you for being so helpful.**

Bank official : **Please don't mention it, ma'am. It's my duty.**

DIALOGUE 3

(Francis asks a passenger in his train compartment to take care of his luggage for a short while.)

Francis : **I hate to trouble you, but would you mind** keeping an eye on my suitcase for a while, **please?** I need to speak to the TTE.

Passenger : **No problem at all.**
Francis : **Thank you so much, ma'am. It's very nice of you.**
Passenger : **You're welcome.**

Dialogue 4

(Manju asks a junior colleague to help her with a project report.)

Manju : Amir, **would it be possible for you to help me** draft my project report this evening?

Amir : **I really wish I could've helped, but I'm** leaving after lunch. My mother's arriving from Pune, and I have to receive her at the station. **I'm so sorry.**

Manju : **That's all right.**

Dialogue 5

(Mr Kumar goes to a neighbour to make a phone call.)

Mr Kumar : Good morning, Mrs Subbaiah. **Could I use your telephone, please.**

Mrs Subbaiah : **I'm afraid**[13.5] our phone's not working since yesterday, Mr Kumar. **But if it's urgent, you could use my son's mobile.**

Mr Kumar : **Thank you, but** it's really not so important. I'll wait until I get to office.

Activity 1

Listen again to dialogues 1–5 and repeat each line for practice.

Listen carefully to the dialogues below and follow them in the book. They are requests made in informal contexts where a person is talking to a friend, relative or neighbour. Again, note that when we are not able to agree to a request, we must turn it down politely.

[13.5] The expression *I'm afraid* ... is another way of saying *I'm sorry* ... . It does not mean that the speaker is actually afraid of something.

DIALOGUE 6

(Savita has to leave for Mumbai urgently. She requests her friend Asha to book her ticket.)

Savita : Asha, my mother has fractured her leg. I have to leave for Mumbai tonight. **Sorry to bother you, but could you please** book a ticket for me on the Goa Express leaving this evening.

Asha : **Sure.** If it's not available (or If I can't get one), **can I** get you a *tatkal* ticket?

Savita : **Yes, please.**

Asha : **I'll** go **right away**. You see to the packing.

Savita : **Thanks so much**, Asha. **I knew I could ask you for help.**

Asha : **You don't have to thank me**, Savita. **That's what friends are for,** aren't they? Bye.

Savita : Bye.

DIALOGUE 7

(Sarala asks her nephew to help her with a heavy suitcase.)

Sarala : Naveen, **would you help me** put this suitcase on the shelf? I can't lift it. It's too heavy.

Naveen : **Sure,** auntie. **I'll do it for you.** (*Puts the suitcase on the shelf.*) **There you are.**

Sarala : **Thanks**, Naveen. **You're a great help**.

Naveen : **Anytime,** auntie. **Always happy to help you**.

Sarala : A glass of orange juice for your trouble?

Naveen : I'd love that. Thanks.

DIALOGUE 8

(Hari is riding his motorbike. He sees Jose at the bus stop.)

Jose : Hi, Hari. Where're you going?

Hari : I'm going to the market.

Jose : **Can you give me a lift to** the bus stop, **please.**

Hari : **Okay**! Hop on.

Jose : Thanks.

DIALOGUE 9

(Sudhir asks his cousin Amita to go shopping with him.)

Sudhir : Amita, **will you** come shopping with me this evening, **please**? I have to buy a present for mother. It's her birthday next week.

Amita : **I'm sorry I can't** make it today, Sudhir. **I have my** music class. **But I'd love to help you** choose a gift for auntie. **Can we** go tomorrow evening **instead?**

Sudhir : **Oh, yes. We could do that.** See you tomorrow evening then. Bye.

Amita : Bye.

DIALOGUE 10

(Vinu asks his friend Praveen to take care of his dog for two days while he is out of town.)

Vinu : Praveen, **could you do me a favour**[13.10], **please. Could you** take care of my dog while I'm away.

Praveen : I **really wish I could, but** I'm going to my village for a week. **Sorry about not being able to help**.

Vinu : **That's okay. I'll think of** someone else.

13.10 Say 'Do me a favour, please' (very informal), 'Could you do me a favour, please' or 'I'd like to ask a favour of you' (formal), and *not* 'Could you do a favour for me, please' or 'I want a favour from you.'

Praveen : Hey! Why don't you ask Kamala? College is closed for summer vacation, and she loves Babu anyway. I don't think she'd mind.

Vinu : Thanks. That's a good idea. I'll speak to Kamala.

Useful points to remember

- Requests can be either direct (as in *Could I use your telephone, please)* or indirect (as in *Would it be possible for you to draft my project report?)*
- When making a request, remember that *Would you*...? or *Could you*...? are more formal than *Will you*...? or *Can you?*
- One way of making a request more polite is by starting with an apology (as in *Sorry to bother you, but could you book a ticket for me?*)
- When agreeing to a request, you can show that you are doing so willingly by using *I'd be happy to* / *I'd be glad to* / *Certainly* / *Yes, of course* / *My pleasure*.
- When declining a request, you can show that you regret not being able to agree by using expressions such as *I'm sorry, but* . . . and *I wish I could have, but* . . . . You can also indicate that you are concerned about the problem of the person making the request by offering alternative solutions or making helpful suggestions (as in *Can we go tomorrow instead?*)

ACTIVITY 2

Listen again to dialogues 6–10 and repeat each line for practice.

Look at the list of expressions you could use to make and respond to a request. The expressions at the top are more formal than those towards the bottom of the list.

Use these to make a request	Use these to respond
May I request you to . . . , please.*	I consider it a privilege to . . . .*
	I feel honoured to . . . .*
	I would like to thank . . . for . . . .

(contd...)

* These expressions are used only in very formal situations.

I was wondering if you'd do me a favour.	My pleasure.
I'd be grateful if you could . . .	Certainly.
I'd really appreciate it if you'd . . .	I'd be delighted.
If you don't mind, could you . . ., please.	I'd be happy to.
Could I ask a favour of you, please.	Of course.
I wonder if you could . . . ?	I'd be glad to.
Do you think it would be possible for you to . . .?	No problem at all.
Do you think you could . . .?	Sure.
Would it be possible for you to . . . ?	Okay.
Would you mind . . .?	

Sorry to bother you, but could you . . ., please.

I hate to trouble you, but could you . . ., please.

Would you . . . , please.

Could you . . . , please.

Can you . . . , please.

ACTIVITY 3

Fill in the blanks with suitable expressions. You can use the expressions that appear in bold in the sample dialogues. The first blank is filled for you, as an example. Listen to the CD to check your answers, but remember that in some cases there could be more than one acceptable answer.

Requests	Responses
a. <u>Could you </u>do me a favour, please.	a. <u>I'd be glad to</u>.
b. .... carry these books for me to the library?	b. ....

(contd...)

c. Hey, Rama, can you help me with the physics problems?	c. I'm afraid ...., Arjun. .... (*give a reason*)
d. ....take baby out for a while?	d. I'd love to.
e. ....the chairperson to deliver her inaugural address.	e. I feel .... to address this learned audience.
f. I was wondering .... pick up my blouses from the tailor on your way back from school.	f. .... But I have to go to the computer class today, and that's in the other direction.

PAIR WORK

ACTIVITY 4

Enact dialogues 1–10 with a partner.

ACTIVITY 5

Enact the completed exchanges in activity 3 with your partner.

ACTIVITY 6 →

Working in pairs, complete the short exchanges below, consisting of requests and responses (positive/negative). You can use the words in the boxes and add others of your own to fill in the gaps in the outlines. After you have completed the dialogues, enact them with your partner.

a. Mrs Shekhar asks Smita to buy a kurta for her son Amit. (informal)

Mrs Shekhar : .... Amit.
Smita : .... I'd...................., auntie.
Mrs Shekhar : ....
Smita : ....

sure	can	any time	thanks	love to

b. Rajiv asks Arun to help him decorate the stage for a dance programme. (informal)

Rajiv : .... you .... staying back to .... the dance programme?

Arun : I ...., but I ....home early today.

Rajiv : That's ....

Arun : .... for understanding.

would	thanks	okay	mind	wish I could have	to be

c. The physical instructor asks the head of the sports department to help him plan the schedule for Sports Day. (formal)

Physical instructor : If it's ...., ...?

Head : ....

Physical instructor : .... so much.

Head : My ....

pleasure	certainly	not too much trouble	thank you

d. The headmaster requests the chief guest, the Education Minister, to inaugurate the new science block and to address the gathering. (very formal)

Headmaster : .... I now .... the Hon'ble Education Minister .... the new science block and .... the gathering.

Minister : I'm .... to be .... here this morning, and .... to speaking to you.

look forward	delighted	may	present	request

GROUP WORK

ACTIVITY 7 →

Rewrite dialogue 9 by changing the situation, but retaining the expressions used to make and respond to a request. For example, you could begin the dialogue with: *Amita, will* you come *to the Dussehra celebrations with me this evening, please?* Each pair can then enact its dialogue before the group.

MODULE 3

UNIT 14

ASKING FOR DIRECTIONS AND GIVING DIRECTIONS

If you do not know the way to a place, you usually ask someone how to get there. You also have to explain how to reach a place if someone asks you the way. This unit will help you learn how to ask politely for and give clear directions in English. Note that whether you are talking to complete strangers or to people whom you know, there is not much difference in the kind of language you will use to ask for and give directions.

एखाद्या ठिकाणी जायचा रस्ता माहीत नसला की तुम्ही साधारणपणे कोणालातरी तेथे कसे जायचे ते विचारता. कोणी तुम्हाला पत्ता विचारला की तेथे कसे जायचे हे तुम्हालाही कोणालातरी समजावून सांगावे लागते. इंग्लिशमधून नम्रपणे पत्ता कसा विचारावा किंवा कसा समजावून सांगावा हे या पाठात शिकता येईल. लक्षात ठेवा की पत्ता विचारताना किंवा समजावून सांगताना तुम्ही अगदी अनोळखी व्यक्तीशी बोलत असलात किंवा ओळखीच्या व्यक्तीशी तरी तुमच्या भाषेत फारसा फरक पडत नाही.

Listen to the dialogues below and follow them in the book.

DIALOGUE 1

(Ratan is a new student in the college. He asks Varun for directions to the library.)

Ratan : **Excuse me, could you tell me the way to the** library?

Varun : **Sure. Go straight down this path** and **you'll reach the** new block. **To the left of the** reception desk **is a** staircase. **Go up the stairs to the** second **floor and turn right**. **You will find** the library **at the end of the** floor.

Ratan : **Thanks a lot.**

Varun : **You're welcome.**

DIALOGUE 2

(Asma calls Bharat from the bus depot, asking for directions to his house.)

Asma : (on the phone) Hi, Bharat.

Bharat : Oh, hi, Asma! Where're you calling from?

Asma : From the Saket bus depot. **How do I get to** your house?

Bharat : **First, turn right, then turn left and walk down**[14.2] the road **until you come to the traffic lights at the crossroads. There, take the right turn. Got it?**

Asma : **Yes. And then**?

Bharat : **Keep walking till you see** the Shubham Hotel **on your left. Right opposite** the hotel **is a lane leading to** my house. **It's the second** house **in the lane. There's a** big mango tree **in the** garden. **Okay?**

Asma : Yes, thanks. I'll be there soon. See you.

DIALOGUE 3

(Paul asks a passerby where he can find a stationery shop.)

Paul : **Excuse me, would you mind telling me where I can find** a stationery shop **here**?

Passerby : **Not at all. Turn left at** the chemist's, **go down the road** and **take the second right. Walk on till you reach** Ganesh department store. **The** stationer's **is the third shop from** the department store.

Paul : **Third shop from** the department store?

[14.2] The sentences *Walk up the road* and *Walk down the road* do not always mean that the road is sloping up or down. We usually use the sentences to mean *Walk along the road.*

Passerby : **Yes, that's right.**
Paul : **Thank you so much.**
Passerby : **You're welcome.**

DIALOGUE 4

(Reena wants Suma to work with her on a project at the weekend. But Suma does not know the way to Reena's house.)

Reena : Could you come home on Saturday, Suma? We can work on the science project.
Suma : I can come, Reena, **but I don't know the way**.
Reena : **I'll tell you how to get here**. **Take** bus number 9 **from** Tarnaka. **Get off at** Shanti cinema. **Right opposite the** cinema **is** Sharada Apartments. **Walk in and take the lift** to the second floor. **Our flat is** B 6.
Suma : That's easy. See you at ten, then.
Reena : Okay.

Here are some more expressions you can use to ask directions and to give them:

Asking for directions	Giving directions
1. **Can you tell me where** the Bata shoe shop **is?**	1. **It's opposite** the State Bank of Hyderabad, **next to** the Kamath Hotel.
2. **Could you direct me to** the principal's office, **please?**	2. **Go along the** corridor and **turn left. It's just round the corner**.
3. **How far is** the Navrang theatre **from here?**	3. **It's about a** three-minute walk **from here**. **Cross the** road and **go straight on**.
4. **Can you help me find** the bus pass counter, **please?**	4. **It's on the other side** (of this bus stand), **near the** main entrance, **facing the** fresh fruit juice stall. **You can't miss it.**

(contd...)

5. **Can you show me the way to** the Skyline cinema?

5. **It's in** Basheer Bagh. **From** the crossing, **go towards** Hussain Sagar. **On your right, you'll see** the Shanbagh. **Take the lane next to** the hotel and **walk down it about** ten **yards. You'll see** Skyline **on your left. You can't miss it.**

6. **Excuse me, is this** Shivaji Park?

6. **No, I'm afraid you've come to the wrong place. This is** Shivaji Nagar. Shivaji Park **is at the other end of the** city, **near** the Secretariat.

ACTIVITY 1 →

Listen again to dialogues 1–4 and repeat each line for practice.

PAIR WORK

ACTIVITY 2 →

Working in pairs, change the situation in dialogue 1 and rewrite it using any of the expressions in bold letters to ask for and give directions. You can, for example, begin the dialogue like this: *Excuse me, could you tell me the way to <u>the canteen</u>?* After you finish writing the dialogue, enact it with your partner, taking turns so that each of you plays the two roles.

Ratan : ....

Varun : ....
....
....
....

Ratan : ....

Varun : ....

ACTIVITY 3

Fill in the blanks in the dialogue with any one of the expressions given in brackets. All the expressions would be acceptable. After you complete the dialogue, enact it with your partner, taking turns so that each of you plays the two roles.

Namita : Excuse me,................................ (*could you tell me the way / which is the way / how do I get*) to the Gandhi Nagar bus stop?

Anandi : Go ....(*straight / till the traffic lights*), then................(*take the first right turn / turn to your left*) and the bus stop is.................(*next to / in front of / opposite*) the Taj Hotel.

Namita : Thank you so much. It's really kind of you to help.

Anandi : Not at all. You're welcome.

ACTIVITY 4

Working in pairs, complete the dialogue below, in which Vincent gives Anand directions to reach his house for lunch. Use some of the expressions you have learnt in this unit to complete it. After you finish, compare it with the dialogue you will hear on CD and enact it with your partner.

Vincent : I hope you're coming over to my place for lunch tomorrow.

Anand : Of course, I am. But I'm not sure if I know the way to your house. ....

Vincent : ....

Anand : Thanks. That sounds simple. I think I'll be able to find my way.

ACTIVITY 5

There are two maps A and B below, each with two routes that could be taken to go from Start Nagar to Finish Colony. Working in pairs, choose a map each, and first mark one of the routes and then give your partner clear directions to take that route to Finish Colony. Your partner will mark the

route you give in his/ her book. Compare your map with your partner's to check if the two routes match. Next your partner will give you directions, and you can mark the route in the second map. Again, follow the steps explained above.

Map A

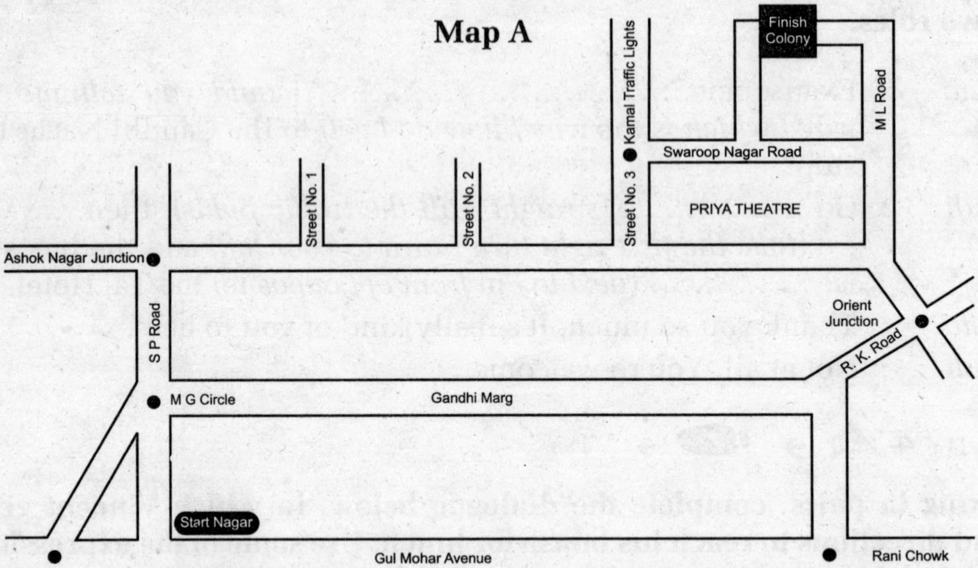

Map B

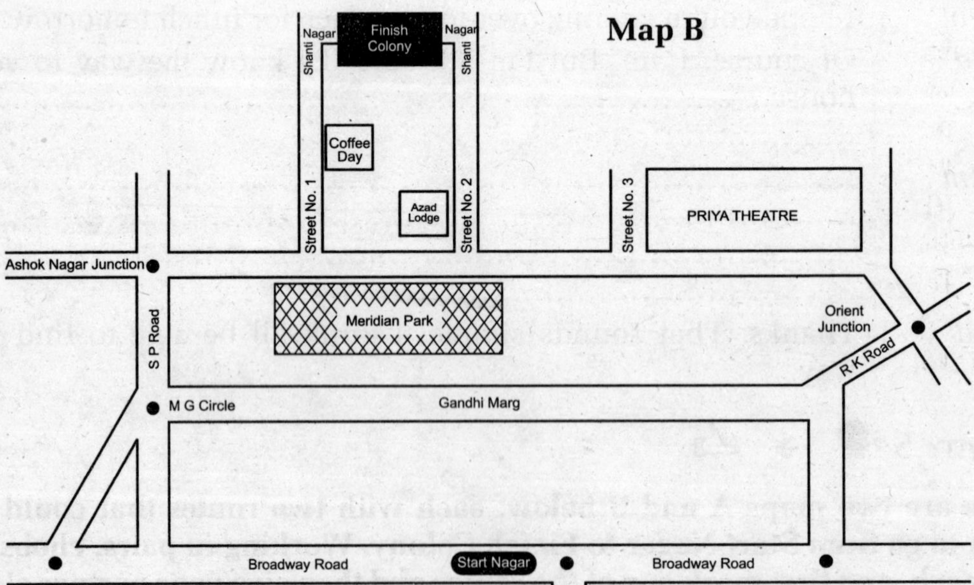

GROUP WORK

ACTIVITY 6

Form groups of five. In the map below, there are five different routes you can take to go from the Vocational Training College to the Lotus Lake. Work together and mark the five routes on the map using the numbers 1–5. Each member of the group can choose one route. He/she can then first write down and then tell the others in the group how to get to the lake by that route. After everyone has finished, compare the directions you gave with what you hear on CD.

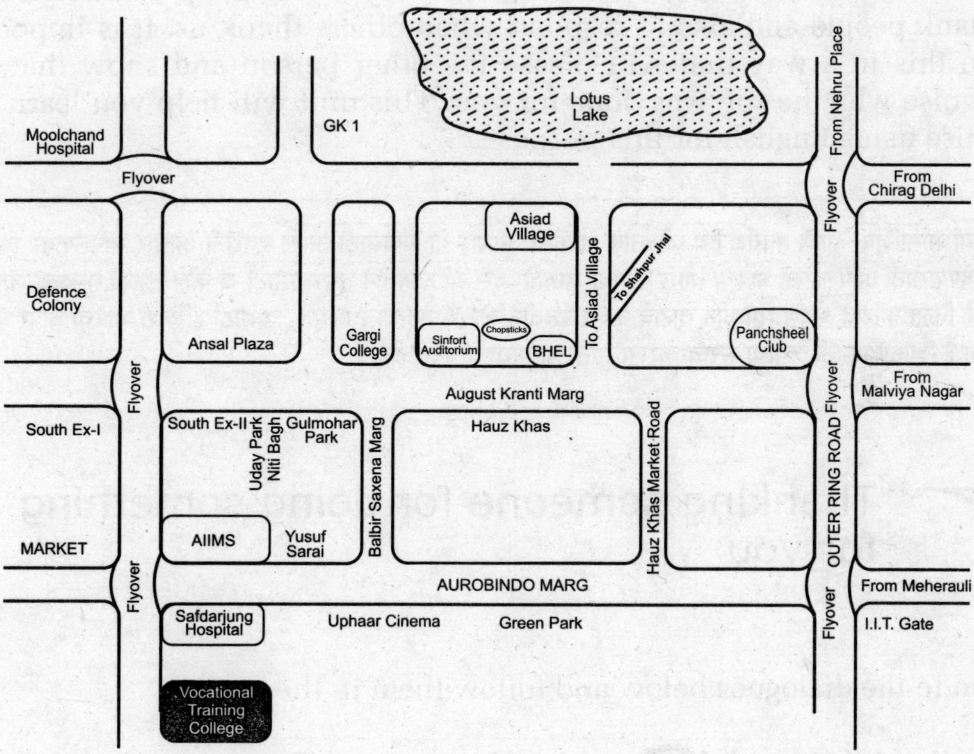

MODULE 3

UNIT 15

THANKING SOMEONE AND RESPONDING TO THANKS

We often need to use language in our everyday social and professional lives to thank people and also to respond when others thank us. It is important to do this in a way that will please the other person and show that you recognise what he/she was done for you. This unit will help you learn and practise using English for this purpose.

रोजच्या सामाजिक आणि कार्यक्षेत्रीय जीवनात लोकांचे आभार मानण्यासाठी आणि इतरांनी आभार मानल्यावर त्याला उत्तर देण्यासाठी आपल्याला भाषेचा वापर करावा लागतो. दुसऱ्या व्यक्तीने तुमच्यासाठी जे केले त्याची तुम्हाला जाणीव आहे हे तिला कळावे आणि समाधान वाटावे अशा पद्धतीने बोलणे महत्त्वाचे असते. यासाठी इंग्लिश भाषेचा वापर कसा करावा हे शिकण्यासाठी, त्याचा सराव करण्यासाठी या पाठाची मदत होईल.

a Thanking someone for doing something for you

Listen to the dialogues below and follow them in the book.

DIALOGUE 1 (FORMAL)

(Rajini and Salim thank their teacher after they get back from a class trip.)

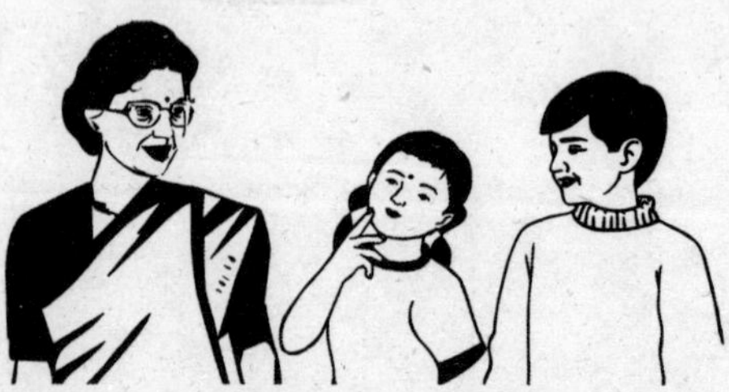

Teacher : Are you happy we went to Osman Sagar?

Rajini : Oh, **we had a wonderful time**, ma'am.

Salim : **It was a great** picnic. **Thank you for taking such good care of us.**

Teacher : **I'm glad you enjoyed yourselves**. I had a good time too.

DIALOGUE 2 (FORMAL)

(Mrs Venkat is waiting at a bus stop with a junior colleague. Someone snatches her handbag and runs away. Her colleague runs after the man and gets the handbag back. Mrs Venkat thanks him for the help.)

Prabhu : Here's your bag, Mrs Venkat.

Mrs Venkat : Prabhu, **I can't thank you enough for** acting quickly. **If you hadn't** run after him, **I'm sure I'd have** lost my bag.

Prabhu : **I'm glad I could be of help**. Oh, there's your bus, Mrs Venkat. Goodbye!

Mrs Venkat : Bye, and again, **thank you so much.**

Prabhu : **You're welcome**, ma'am.

DIALOGUE 3 (INFORMAL)

(Uma thanks her neighbour Tina for taking care of her baby for a while.)

Uma : Tina, I'm back from the market. **Thanks for** taking care of Neha while I was away.

Tina : Oh, **it was a pleasure**.

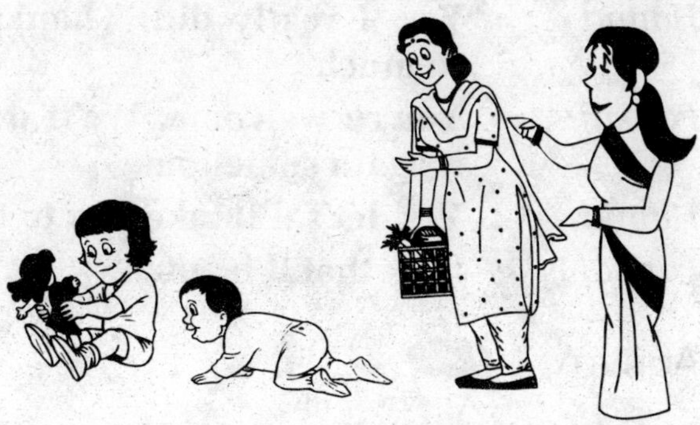

Uma : **Hope** she **was not a problem?**

Tina : **Not at all.** She had lunch, played with Rahul and has had a nap too.

Uma : **Thanks again**, Tina.

Tina : **You're welcome**.

ACTIVITY 1

Listen again to dialogues 1–3 on CD and repeat each line for practice.

b Thanking someone at the end of a meal or party you have been invited to

DIALOGUE 4 (FORMAL)

(Bindu thanks her boss before leaving a party at his house.)

Bindu : I think I should be leaving now, Mr Prasad. **Thank you very much for inviting me to** the party. **It was a lovely evening.**

Mr Prasad : **I'm glad you enjoyed yourself**, Bindu. **Do come again.**

Bindu : **I'd love to. Thank you very much.** Good night.

Mr Prasad : Good night.

DIALOGUE 5 (INFORMAL)

(Hamid thanks his friend after lunch at a restaurant.)

Hamid : Oh, I'll have to run! It's three o'clock. Pankaj, **that was a great treat.**

Pankaj : **I'm happy you liked the place and the food.**

Hamid : **Yes, I really did. Thanks so much.**

Pankaj : **You're welcome. We'll do it again sometime.**

Hamid : **Yes, let's. I'll take you to** the new coffee shop near the beach.

Pankaj : Hey, **that'll be nice!**

ACTIVITY 2

Listen again to dialogues 4 and 5 on CD and repeat each line for practice.

C Thanking someone for a gift

DIALOGUE 6 (FORMAL)

(Shailu thanks the director of her company for his New Year gift.)

Shailu : Good afternoon, Mr Sharma.

Mr Sharma : Good afternoon, Shailu.

Shailu : Sir, **I'd like to thank you for the** planner you sent me. **It really helps me** work more efficiently.

Mr Sharma : It's something I picked up from Mumbai when I went there last week. **I'm glad you find it useful.**

Shailu : I do, sir. **Thank you so much.**

Mr Sharma : **You're welcome**, Shailu.

DIALOGUE 7 (INFORMAL)

(Kaveri thanks her friend for his birthday gift.)

Kaveri : **Thanks a lot for** the painting, Sudhir. **It has** brightened up my room.

Sudhir : **My pleasure. I'm so glad you like it.**

Kaveri : **Why don't you** come home and see how good it looks?

Sudhir : I sure will. **Thanks.**

ACTIVITY 3

Listen again to dialogues 6 and 7 on CD and repeat each line for practice.

Useful points to remember

- ✎ When you thank someone, it is nice to add a positive comment such as *It has brightened up my room* or *It was a lovely evening* or *We had a lovely time.*
- ✎ When someone thanks you, you could respond with more than just *You're welcome* or *My pleasure.* For example, you could say *I'm glad you enjoyed yourself* or *I'm happy you liked the place.*
- ✎ You could repeat expressions of thanks if you want to emphasise just how thankful you are. For example, you could say *Thanks for helping me with my chemistry project. Thanks so much.*
- ✎ You can also express your gratitude by offering to return a favour or a good turn. For example, *I'll take you to the new coffee shop near the beach* or *Why don't you come home and see how good it looks*?

Here are a few other ways of thanking people. Some of them are direct and use the words *Thanks* or *Thank you,* while others are indirect ways of expressing gratitude.

Situations	Expressions of thanks
1. for a gift	1. **Thank you so much for the** book. **I love** detective stories.
2a. when accepting an offer of help	2a. I'm very grateful to you for **taking me to the hospital. I don't think I could've** gone alone.
2b. when refusing an offer of help	2b. **Thanks, but** I think I can manage.
3. in response to a wish	3. **Thank you very much. I really need your good wishes for** my exams.
4a. when accepting an invitation	4a. **It's nice of you to invite me to** your party. **I'll look forward to it.**

(contd...)

4b. when refusing an invitation	4b. **I'd love to come to** your party, **but** I have to take my mother to a music concert. **Thanks anyway for inviting me.** (It is polite to give a reason when we cannot accept an invitation. You will see this in a later unit.)
5. to a person who accepts your invitation	5. **I really appreciate the trouble you've taken to** be here today. **Thank you for coming to the** reception. (formal)
6. when thanking someone at a public function	6. **I take this opportunity to thank . . . . / It's my privilege to propose a vote of thanks** . . . (very formal)

Here are some more expressions you can use to respond when someone thanks you:

You're always welcome.

Don't mention it.

The pleasure's mine. (formal)

It gives me great pleasure to . . . . (very formal)

PAIR WORK

ACTIVITY 4

Enact dialogues 1–7 with a partner, taking turns to play the roles of the person expressing thanks and the one responding to it.

ACTIVITY 5 →

Rewrite the first two lines of dialogue 7, keeping the highlighted expressions but changing the reason for thanking. For example, you could say: *Thanks a lot for the handbag, Sudhir, It's just what I needed. My pleasure. I'm so glad you like it.* After you finish, enact the dialogue with your partner.

ACTIVITY 6

Complete the dialogues below with the lines spoken by the persons expressing thanks or by others responding to them. Compare your dialogues with those that you will hear on CD and enact them with your partner.

a. *Secretary* : *Dr Rajaram, I'd like to take this opportunity to thank you for accepting our invitation to inaugurate the new auditorium.*

Dr Rajaram : ....

b. *Student* : ....

Teacher : You're welcome, Babu. I was happy to help you prepare for the debate. I'm glad you did so well. Congratulations!

c. *Annie* : Thanks for the lovely dupatta you got me from Chandigarh, Rehana. It's really so sweet of you.

Rehana : ....

d. *Nitish* : .... to my sister's wedding.

Ramesh : My pleasure, Nitish. Everything went so well!

e. *Mrs Nair* : .... me a lift, Balan. Without your help, ... reached the station on time.

Balan : ...., auntie. ....

GROUP WORK

ACTIVITY 7

Form groups of five or six. The teacher will make slips, each having the number of one of the outlines below. The number of slips will be the same as the number of groups in the class. Pick from the teacher's desk one of the folded slips of paper. Use the outline matching the number on your slip to write a dialogue. Each group can enact its dialogue before the class.

a. Shilpa meets Fatima after her wedding.

Shilpa's lines	Fatima's lines
i. Thanks her for the wedding gift (mention the gift)	i. Responds to Shilpa's thanks.
ii. Says why she likes it.	ii. Says she's glad Shilpa liked the gift.
iii. Invites her home.	iii. Thanks Shilpa for inviting her home.
iv. Says goodbye.	iv. Responds.

b. Santosh gets ready to leave his friend Jai's house after staying with him for a month.

Santosh's lines	Jai's lines
i. Thanks Jai for the lovely stay he had.	i. Says that it was great having him and that he is glad Santosh enjoyed the visit.
ii. Says how much he enjoyed the food, the outings and the fun he had with Jai's parents and brother.	ii. Says everyone in his family would miss him too.
iii. Invites Jai to visit him during the summer vacation.	iii. Thanks Santosh for the invitation.
iv. Says that it is time to leave for the bus depot and bids goodbye.	iv. Responds.

c. Joseph's daughter had to miss classes for two months because of an illness. He thanks the principal of his daughter's college for allowing her to take the final exams on submission of a medical certificate for the period.

Joseph's lines	Principal's lines
i. Greets the principal and asks her if his daughter, Ritu, would be allowed to take the final exams.	i. Returns the greeting and says that Ritu could take the exams after submitting a medical certificate from the doctor who had treated her.

(contd...)

ii. Thanks the principal for granting Ritu permission to take the exams.	ii. Says that it is all right because Ritu had been too ill to attend college.
iii. Promises to send the medical certificate in two days time.	ii. Says that that would be fine.
iv. Takes leave.	iv. Responds.

MODULE 4

UNIT 16 INVITING, AND ACCEPTING AND REFUSING AN INVITATION

There are times when you need to invite people to a party, a reception, a wedding, or a birthday or anniversary celebration. You also need to know how to say that you will or will not be able to accept an invitation when someone invites you. This unit will help you to learn and practise doing this in English.

काही वेळा तुम्हाला मेजवानी, स्वागत समारंभ, विवाह, वाढदिवस, वार्षिक समारंभ यांसाठी लोकांना निमंत्रण द्यायचे असते. कोणी तुम्हाला निमंत्रण दिले तर आपण ते स्वीकारू शकतो की नाही हे कसे सांगायचे हेही तुम्हाला माहीत असणे आवश्यक असते. हे इंग्लिशमधून कसे करायचे ते शिकण्यासाठी, त्याचा सराव करण्यासाठी या पाठाची मदत होईल.

a Inviting and accepting an invitation

Listen carefully to the following dialogues on CD and follow them in the book. The situations in which the dialogues take place are all formal.

DIALOGUE 1 (FORMAL)

(Raghu invites a producer to inaugurate a film festival.)

Raghu : Good morning, Ms Nayak. We're organising a children's film festival at the Kalakriti Auditorium. **May I invite you to** inaugurate it.

Meera Nayak : **Thank you very much. That's very kind of you.** When is the inaugural function?

Raghu : **At** ten **o'clock in the** morning **on** 20th June.

Meera Nayak : **That suits me. I'll be there.**

Raghu : **Thank you for accepting our invitation**, Ms Nayak.

Meera Nayak : **My pleasure.**

DIALOGUE 2 (FORMAL)

(Lata invites the police commissioner to be the chief guest at her college annual day celebrations. Time: 12 p.m.)

Lata : Good afternoon, sir. I'm Lata Prasad from the Government Degree College for Women.

Commissioner : Good afternoon, Ms Prasad. What can I do for you?

Lata : We're celebrating our annual day **on** the 16th **on** the college premises. The programme begins at 11 o'clock. **We'd be delighted if you could** be the chief guest.

Commissioner : **Thank you. I'll be happy to be present at the** annual day celebrations.

Lata : **We('re) look(ing) forward to having you with us**, sir.

DIALOGUE 3 (FORMAL)

(Surekha invites her teacher to a house-warming party. The teacher accepts the invitation.)

Surekha : Good morning, ma'am.

Teacher : Good morning, Surekha. You look happy today. Anything special?

Surekha : Yes, ma'am. **We're having a house-warming party at eight o'clock on Sunday in our new flat. Would you be**

able to come for lunch, please? The address is 172, 7th cross, 2nd Block, Jayanagar, near Vijaya College.

Teacher : **I'd love to come,** Surekha. **Thank you.** Shall I be there around one?

Surekha : Yes, ma'am. **It'll be simply wonderful if you could come. Thank you**, ma'am.

Teacher : **You're welcome**, Surekha.

Useful points to remember

- A formal oral invitation is usually accompanied by a written invitation.
- When we invite someone, we usually begin by informing them about the event—i.e. what we are inviting them to— and requesting them to be present on the occasion. (For example, *We're having a . . .*, *I'll be happy to . . .*, *Would you like to come. . .* and *We'd like you to join us.*)
- When we give the details of an event or programme, we usually follow the order (i) time (ii) date and (iii) venue of the programme (*at . . . on/ on the /tomorrow . . . at/in . . .*).
- When someone invites us, it is polite to thank the person. If we accept the invitation, we must express our pleasure in doing so, using expressions such as *Thank you. I'll be happy to be present . . . .*
- After we accept an invitation, we could either ask for the time, date and venue in case the details have not been given or ask for a repetition or clarification in case we did not hear them clearly. To do this, we can use expressions such as *Where, What time, Shall I come around . . . o'clock* and *Could you repeat the address, please.*
- It is also usual to congratulate the person making the invitation if the occasion is that of a celebration, such as a wedding, a birth or a promotion.
- When someone says yes to our invitation, it is polite to thank them. Again, we could express our joy at our invitation being accepted, using expressions such as *We look forward to seeing you.*

Activity 1

Listen again to dialogues 1, 2 and 3 and repeat each line for practice.

PAIR WORK

ACTIVITY 2

Enact the sample dialogues with a partner.

ACTIVITY 3

Fill in the missing parts in the dialogue given below. After you finish, compare your dialogues with those that you will hear on CD and enact them with your partner.

a. *Ahmed* : Good evening, Mr Ramana. I have some good news.

Ramana : Good evening, Mr Ahmed. Please come in.

Ahmed : My son's getting married. The wedding reception .... 7.30 in the evening ...... 25th of July .... Gandhi Park Community Centre. We'd .... if you and your family....................................... come to the reception.

Ramana : Congratulations, Mr Ahmed! We'll ....be there. It'll be ....

Ahmed : Thank you. We'll .... to seeing you on the 25th then.

b. *Mallika* : Good morning, sir. I'm Mallika Raju, secretary of the Vidyanagar Andhra Mahila Samiti.

Minister : Good morning, Ms Raju. What can I do for you?

Mallika : We are holding our annual convention .... 11 .... 14 September .... Samiti Hall .... M. G. Road. .... honoured if you could deliver the inaugural address ...... 10 a.m. .... 11th.

Minister : .... for the invitation. I'll .... deliver the address. I have always admired the work done by your association.

Mallika : .... for accepting our invitation.

Activity 4

Follow the hints below and write a suitable dialogue. After you finish, compare your dialogue with what you will hear on CD. (You can use your own names in the dialogues you write.)

- Your teacher Dr Rama Rao has been transferred to another district.Your class would like to give him a farewell party.
- You invite him to a party.
- You state the time and day of the week.
- Your teacher accepts the invitation.
- You thank him.

Activity 5

Enact the dialogue you have written, taking turns so that each of you plays the two roles.

Listen carefully to the following dialogues on CD and follow them in the book. The situations in which the dialogues take place are informal.

Dialogue 4 (informal)

(Kripa invites her cousin Naresh to join her and her brother on vacation. Naresh accepts the invitation.)

Kripa : **What are you doing during** the winter holidays?

Naresh : Nothing in particular.

Kripa : Amar and I are going on an excursion. **How about coming with us?**

Naresh : **Oh yes, thanks. I'd love to**. Where are you going?

Kripa : Kanyakumari. On our way back, we'll stop over at Thiruvananthapuram for a day.

Naresh : **That'll be lovely.**

Kripa : **I'm glad you'll join us. It'll be fun.**

DIALOGUE 5 (INFORMAL)

(Anasuya invites her colleague to a party arranged on her parents' twenty-fifth anniversary. Aswath agrees to be present.)

Anasuya : Aswath, **we're having a party to celebrate** my parents' silver anniversary. **It's at** 7.30 tomorrow evening **at** the Hotel Sangeet. **Would you be able to come?**

Aswath : **Sure. D'you need any help?**

Anasuya : Thanks, but no. My husband's made all the arrangements. We are having a vocal music recital followed by dinner.

Aswath : **That sounds great.** I have a sales meeting now. See you later.

Anasuya : See you.

DIALOGUE 6 (INFORMAL)

(Subrahmanya invites his friend Raghava to the inauguration of a public health centre in his village. Raghava accepts the invitation.)

Subrahmanya : Hi, Raghava. Can you come with us to our village tomorrow? **I want you to attend the opening ceremony of a public health centre on Sunday morning at ten.** My grandfather, who is one of the elders of the village, is inaugurating it.

Raghava : **That sounds great,** Subri. **Thank you. I'd love to come. When are we leaving?**

Subrahmanya : My father said we should leave very early tomorrow morning. Can you stay with us tonight? **It'll be fun**!

Raghava : I guess I can.

Subrahmanya : Good. See you then.

Raghava : Bye.

Useful points to remember

- When inviting friends or people whom you know well, you can use expressions such as *How about coming over for . . .* or *How would you like to join us . . .* or *Can you make it?*
- You can accept informal invitations with expressions such as *Sure, I'd love to* or *Great*.
- In informal situations, you can also offer to bring food or some other item or help in some way as, for example, in *What should I bring?* and *Need any help*?

ACTIVITY 6

Listen again to dialogues 4, 5 and 6 and repeat each line for practice.

PAIR WORK

ACTIVITY 7

Enact the sample dialogues with a partner.

ACTIVITY 8

Complete the following exchanges by writing a line to accept each invitation.

a. *A*: I'm going sightseeing on Sunday. Can you also make it?
   B: ....

b. *A*: I'm having a puppet show at home. I'd be happy if you could come.
   B: ....

c. *A*: There's a music competition in the college. May I invite you to be a judge?
   B: ....

d. *A*: We'd be delighted if you could give a talk on your experiences in Singapore.
   B: ....

ACTIVITY 9

Compare the dialogues you have just completed with those that you will hear on CD and enact them with your partner.

GROUP WORK

ACTIVITY 10

Form groups of six. Working in pairs, write a short dialogue each inviting a friend home on a special occasion, such as a festival (for e.g. Deepavali) or a celebration (for e.g. a wedding anniversary). After everyone finishes, each pair can enact its dialogue for the group.

b Declining an invitation*

Listen carefully to the following dialogues on CD and follow them in the book. The situations in which the dialogues take place are formal.

DIALOGUE 7 (FORMAL)

(Kanti invites Professor Madan to judge a contest, but he is not able to accept the invitation.)

Kanti : Good morning, Professor Madan.

Professor : Good morning. Is there anything I can do for you?

Kanti : **We're having an** inter-college debating contest **on** 14th July. **Could I invite you to be a judge, please.**

Professor : **I'd really like to come, but unfortunately I have** another engagement on the 14th.

* When you say no to an invitation, you decline it, or refuse it, or turn it down.

Kanti : **What a disappointment! We were looking forward to having you, but I suppose it can't be helped.**

Professor : **I'm sorry. Perhaps I'll be able to make it next time** you have a debating competition.

Dialogue 8 (formal)

(Nagesh invites his boss to his sister's wedding. The boss has to refuse the invitation.)

Nagesh : Good morning, sir. May I come in?

Boss : Good morning, Nagesh. Please come in. What can I do for you?

Nagesh : Sir, **my sister's getting married on Wednesday. I've come to invite you to the wedding reception. It's from six in the evening at the Raja Kalyana Mandapam in Kukkatpally.**

Boss : **Thank you for the invitation, Nagesh. I wish I could've come, but I'm sorry I won't be able to. I'll be leaving for Bangalore on Tuesday night.**

Nagesh : **I was hoping you'd** be there to bless the newly married couple. **But it doesn't matter. I understand**, sir.

Boss : I wish your sister a very long and happy married life, Nagesh.

Nagesh : Thank you, sir.

Activity 11

Listen again to dialogues 7 and 8 and repeat each line for practice.

PAIR WORK

ACTIVITY 12

Enact the sample dialogues with a partner.

ACTIVITY 13

Complete the dialogues below with suitable responses. After you finish, compare your dialogues with those that you will hear on CD and enact them with your partner.

a. *Namita* : Can you come for lunch on Sunday, Manoj?
Manoj : ....
Namita : Thanks for saying you'll come.

b. *Rahim* : Good morning, Mr Samuel. I'd be happy if you could come to my daughter's dance programme on Saturday at the Sarvakala Bhavan.
Samuel : I'd love to. ....?
Rahim : At six in the evening.

c. *Rajesh* : I'm going to my uncle's farm house for Sankranti. I want you to join me if you're free.
Chandra : Oh, I'm ...., but ....complete my science project.
Rajesh : What a shame! I was hoping you'd be able to make it.

Listen carefully to the following dialogues on CD and follow them in the book. The situations in which the dialogues take place are informal.

DIALOGUE 9 (INFORMAL)

(Joseph invites his neighbour to join a family outing.)

Joseph : We're going to the zoo on Sunday. Would you like to come?
Renu : Sorry, **but I have to go to a** wedding.
Joseph : **What a pity! We'll miss you.**

Renu : (Do) tell me all about it on Monday.

Joseph : Sure. Bye!

Renu : Bye!

DIALOGUE 10 (INFORMAL)

(Vishal invites his classmate Abdul to his niece's naming ceremony. Abdul has to refuse the invitation.)

Vishal : Abdul, **it's my niece's naming ceremony tomorrow morning. Can you come home by eight?**

Abdul : Vishal, **you know how eagerly I've been waiting for the occasion. I would've loved to come but** my grandmother is in hospital, and I must be with her. **What a shame I can't come! Thanks, anyway.** I'll come and see the baby another day.

Vishal : **It would've been nice if you were there**, Abdul. **But don't worry**. Your grandmother needs you.

Useful points to remember

When we have to refuse an invitation, we do it politely by

- expressing our thanks, as in *Thanks for the invitation.*
- apologising for being unable to accept it, as in *I would've been glad to come, but I'm sorry I can't.*
- giving a reason for refusing it, as in *I'll be leaving for* ....

ACTIVITY 14

Listen again to dialogues 9 and 10 and repeat each line for practice.

PAIR WORK

ACTIVITY 15

Enact the sample dialogues with a partner.

You can use the expressions below to invite people, and to accept and decline invitations. Some of them appear in the sample dialogues while the others are additional ones that you can practise using.

Inviting

formal	informal
I'd/We'd be delighted if you could . . .	How would you like to . . .?
Please . . .	Do you (spoken as d'you) think you'd like to join us?
Would you like to join us/come?	Can you make it?
May I/we invite you to . . .?	How about coming/going . . .?
I'd/ We'd like you to . . .?	I/We want you to . . .
Would you be free to join . . .?	Are you free?
I'd like to invite you to . . .	How about a . . .?
We'd love to have you over for . . .	
We'd be pleased to have you over . . .	
We'll be happy to have you . . .	
We'd be delighted to have you . . .	
We'd be happy if you can come . . .	
It would give us great pleasure to invite you to . . .	

Accepting invitations

formal	informal
Thank you. I'd love to. What time?	Sure. When?/What time?
Thank you. I'll be happy to . . .	I'd love to. What should I bring?
Thank you so much. We'd be delighted to . . .	That sounds like fun. Do you need any help?
We'd be very happy to come . . .	Thanks for asking us. /Great/. I'll be there.
We'd be pleased to attend . . . Thank you for inviting us.	
That would be wonderful . . . Thanks.	

Declining invitations

formal	informal
I'd love to, but I have another engagement/something else on.	Sorry, but I don't think I can make it.
I'd really like to, but unfortunately I'm busy then.	Sorry, but I don't think I'm free.
I'm afraid I'm going to be out of town/ I have to . . .	Oh, that's bad. I already have plans.
Wish I could've come but . . . Thanks all the same.	
I wish I could, but I'm sorry I can't . . . Thanks for inviting me.	
Thank you very much but I'm sorry I can't accept your invitation. I . . .	

GROUP WORK

ACTIVITY 16

Form groups of six. Working in pairs, choose two dialogues each and fill in the blanks in them, using some of the expressions learnt in the unit. Remember to differentiate between formal and informal expressions. For practice, you can make the invitees first accept and then decline the invitation.

a. *(Mr Thyagaraj invites Mrs Venkatesulu and family to his daughter's engagement.)*

Mr Thygarajan : .... to Radha's engagement at eleven o' clock on the twelfth of this month. Will you please come and bless the couple?

Mrs Venkatesulu : ....
.... (*accept*)
....
....
.... (*decline, saying sorry and giving reason*)

b. *(Babu invites his cousin to the annual convocation in his college.)*

Babu : Hey, Raju. .... to the convocation at our college at 4 p.m. on Saturday?

Raju : ....
.... (*accept*)
....
.... (*decline*)

c. *(Mrs Prasad invites a neighbour to her house-warming.)*

Mrs Prasad : We're having a house-warming party at eight o'clock on Sunday morning. We'd ....

Neighbour : ....
.... (*accept*)
....
.... (*decline*)

d. *(Ravi invites his friend John to see a film.)*

Ravi : How .... to see a film on Saturday?

John : ....
.... (*accept*)
....
.... (*decline*)

e. *(Mani invites his sister Vinita to a cricket match.)*

Mani : I'm going to watch a cricket match tomorrow. Do you ....?

Vinita : ....
.... (*accept*)
....
.... (*decline*)

f. *(Anand invites the chairman of the state cooperative society to speak at a seminar.)*

Anand : We're having a one-day national seminar. .... our guest speaker.

Chairman : ....
.... (*accept*)
....
.... (*decline*)

ACTIVITY 17

Compare the dialogues you have written with those you will hear on CD and then enact them with your partner before your group, first inviting, then accepting and finally declining the invitations.

MODULE 4

UNIT 17 APOLOGISING AND RESPONDING TO AN APOLOGY

When we apologise to someone, we tell them that we are sorry for doing something we ought not to have done, or for hurting them, or for causing them bother or trouble. In this unit you will learn to use different expressions to say sorry.

कोणाची क्षमायाचना करताना आपण त्यांना आपल्याला वाईट वाटते हे सांगतो. करू नये अशी गोष्ट केली, कोणाला दुखावले, कोणाला त्रास दिला किंवा संकटात टाकले तर आपल्याला त्याबद्दल वाईट वाटते, हे वेगवेगळ्याप्रकारे कसे सांगायचे हे या पाठात शिकता येईल.

Listen carefully to the dialogues below on CD and follow them in the book. The situations in which the dialogues take place are formal.

DIALOGUE 1 (FORMAL)

(Chandran apologises to a senior colleague for not completing his work on time.)

Sheila Bose : Mr Chandran, could we meet this afternoon to discuss your project proposal, please.

Chandran : Ms Bose, **I must apologise** for not complet**ing** the proposal on time. **I was unwell**.

Sheila Bose : **That's all right. But please complete** it by next week.

Chandran : I certainly will.

DIALOGUE 2 (FORMAL)

(Satish apologises to his teacher for talking in class.)

Satish (*at the staff room*) : Excuse me, ma'am.
Teacher : Yes, Satish. What is it?
Satish : Ma'am, **I'm really sorry for** talking in class. Suma wanted to know what we did in the class she missed yesterday. But **I know I shouldn't have been talking**.
Teacher : Satish, you know how annoying it is when you don't pay attention.
Satish : Yes, ma'am, I realise that. **I won't do it again.**
Teacher : **Don't worry about it.**
Satish : **Thank you, ma'am.**

DIALOGUE 3 (FORMAL)

(Sirish apologises to his boss for reaching office late.)

Boss : Where's Sirish?
Revati : He hasn't come in yet, sir. (*Pause*). Oh, here he is.
Sirish : **Excuse me for** being **late**, sir. **The bus didn't turn up, and I had to look for an auto.**
Boss : **That's okay. But please** be on time in future.
Sirish : I will, sir.

ACTIVITY 1

Listen again to dialogues 1, 2 and 3 and repeat each line for practice.

PAIR WORK

ACTIVITY 2

Enact the sample dialogues with a partner.

Listen carefully to the dialogues below on CD and follow them in the book. The situations in the dialogues are informal.

DIALOGUE 4 (INFORMAL)

(Shilpa has to meet her friend Arati, who is coming from Assam, at the railway station. But Shilpa is late by ten minutes.)

Arati : Here you are at last, Shilpa! Hi! I was beginning to get worried.

Shilpa : Hi! Look **I'm really sorry I'm late**. I was caught in a traffic jam.

Arati : **No problem**. It's good to see you.

DIALOGUE 5 (INFORMAL)

(Sharan apologises to his aunt for not getting her a book she wanted.)

Aunt : Have you got me a copy of the Oxford Advanced Learner's Dictionary?

Sharan : **I'm really feeling bad I haven't been able to,** auntie. **Actually** it's in short supply.

Aunt : **Don't let it bother you**, Sharan.

Notice that there is no significant difference between the language used for apologising in formal and in informal situations.

ACTIVITY 3

Listen again to dialogues 4 and 5 and repeat each line for practice.

ACTIVITY 4

Enact the sample dialogues with a partner.

Useful points to remember

- The following expressions are commonly used to apologise or express regret:
  - I must apologise for . . . ing . . . .
  - I'm sorry for (also, *about*) . . . ing . . . .
  - Excuse me for . . . ing . . . .
- Sometimes, after apologising, we accept the blame for the mistake.
  - I know I shouldn't have . . .
  - I realise that it is my fault, but . . .
- Then the reason for something happening for which the apology is being made, is given or a promise made not to repeat an action.
  - I was unwell.
  - Suma wanted to know what you were teaching us.
  - The bus didn't turn up on time.
  - I won't do it again.
- The following expressions are commonly used to accept an apology.
  - That's okay. But . . . (suggesting that something should not happen again).
  - That's all right. These things happen.
  - Don't worry about it.
- Some other expressions you can use to:

make an apology	accept an apology
(I'm) Sorry.	Oh, that's fine.
Please forgive me.	Don't let it bother you. / I understand.
I really feel bad about . . .	Forget about it. / Never mind. / It doesn't matter.

ACTIVITY 5

Fill in the blanks in the following dialogues, using different expressions to apologise. After you finish, compare your dialogues with those that you will hear on CD and enact them with your partner.

a. *A*: .... for disturbing you.
   B: Oh, that's all right.

b. *A*: .... for the delay in returning the books (that) you lent me.
   B: Don't worry about it.

c. *A*: .... not inviting you to my birthday party.
   B: Forget about it.

d. *A*: Oh, ... I've spilt all the ink.
   B: Never mind.

e. *A*: .... for not informing you about the change in the timetable.
   B: Don't let it bother you.

ACTIVITY 6

Fill in the blanks in the dialogues below, giving a reason for a mistake or promising to correct it. After you finish, compare your dialogues with those that you will hear on CD and enact them with your partner. Take turns so that each of you plays the roles of both the person making the apology and the person accepting it.

a. *A*: I'm so sorry I'm late. .... (*give a reason*).
   B: It's okay. But please don't be late in future.

b. *A*: I have to apologise for making so much noise last night. .... (*promise that it won't happen again*).
   B: Oh, that's all right.

c. *A*: I really feel bad about losing your book. .... (*promise to do something to make up for the mistake*).
   B: Don't worry about it.

d. *A*: I must apologise for losing my temper yesterday .... (*accept that it shouldn't have happened*)

B: It's okay. Don't think about it.

ACTIVITY 7

Fill in the blanks in the following dialogues with suitable expressions to accept an apology. After you finish, compare your dialogues with what you will hear on CD and enact them with your partner. Take turns so that each of you plays the two roles.

a. *A*: I'm so sorry I couldn't complete my assignment yesterday. I had a bad headache.

B: .... But make sure you complete it by tomorrow.

b. *A*: Please forgive me for not attending class yesterday. I had to go to the dentist.

B: ....

c. *A*: I'm extremely sorry for breaking your vase.

B: ....

d. *A*: Can you forgive me for hurting you?

B: ....

e. *A*: Sorry about being late for the game. I overslept and didn't know it was five.

B: ....

GROUP WORK

ACTIVITY 8

Form groups of five. Write a dialogue between a teacher and a student to suit the following situation. Each member of the group must give a different reason for not going on the excursion. Two members of the group can enact the dialogue, and when it comes to the point when a reason needs to be

given, the other members can take turns to add their reasons before the end of the dialogue.

- Your college has organised an excursion during the summer holidays.
- You agreed to go on the excursion.
- But you have to cancel your trip at the last minute.
- You apologise to your teacher and give a reason for not being able to go on the excursion.
- The teacher accepts your apology.

MODULE 4

UNIT 18

CONGRATULATING AND RESPONDING TO CONGRATULATIONS

When we hear of someone achieving something remarkable or of something good happening to them, we congratulate them. Similarly, we must also know how to respond when others congratulate us. Here are some ways in which you can do both in English.

कोणी कौतुकास्पद कामगिरी केली, कोणाच्या बाबतीत काही चांगली गोष्ट घडली असे ऐकले की आपण त्यांचे अभिनंदन करतो. त्याचप्रमाणे कोणी आपले अभिनंदन केले तर काय बोलायचे हे आपल्याला माहीत असायला हवे. हे दोन्ही तुम्ही इंग्लिशमधून कसे करू शकाल याचे काही मार्ग येथे दिले आहेत.

Listen carefully to the dialogues below on CD and follow them in the book.

DIALOGUE 1 (FORMAL)

(Teja has topped his class in the first year Intermediate exams. His teacher congratulates him.)

Teacher : **Congratulations on your wonderful performance**, Teja!
Teja : **Thank you, sir.**

DIALOGUE 2 (INFORMAL)

(Later, Teja's classmate congratulates him.)

Priya : **Congrats**, Teja!
Teja : **Thanks.**

DIALOGUE 3 (FORMAL)

(The college cricket team has won the annual inter-college tournament. The principal congratulates them at a function to honour them. The captain responds.)

Principal : **I must congratulate** the college cricket team on winning the state-level tournament. **We are proud of you and wish you greater success in the future.**

Captain : On behalf of the team, **I thank you**, sir, **for your congratulations and good wishes**.

DIALOGUE 4 (FORMAL)

(Pratibha has got a seat in the Government Engineering College. Mr Govindaraj, her neighbour, congratulates her.)

Mr Govindaraj : We heard you've been admitted to the electrical engineering BTech course, Pratibha. **Congratulations! We're very proud of you.**

Pratibha : **Thank you very much**, uncle. You've always been so encouraging.

DIALOGUE 5 (INFORMAL)

(Manjunath has won a music competition. His friend, Harinder, congratulates him.)

Harinder : **Well done,** Manju! **I knew you'd win the** competition. **I'm so happy for you**.

Manjunath : **Thanks,** Hari. I was a little nervous at the beginning, but I became confident as I started singing.

Useful points to remember

- *Congratulations!* / *Congrats!* and *Thanks* work as a fixed formula for they always go together.
- Do not say *Congratulations for . . .*, but *Congratulations on . . . .*
- We sometimes congratulate people, usually in informal situations, without using the word *Congratulations* in any of its forms (for example, *Well done*.)
- Other expressions that can be used to offer congratulations are:
  May we congratulate you on . . .? (formal)
  We'd like to congratulate . . . (formal)
  Congratulations on your remarkable / wonderful performance.
- Expressions such as *I knew you'd do it*, *We're happy for you* and *I'm proud of you* are often used to emphasise the words *Congratulations* or *Congrats*.

ACTIVITY 1

Listen again to dialogues 1 to 5 and repeat each line for practice.

PAIR WORK

ACTIVITY 2

Enact the sample dialogues with a partner.

ACTIVITY 3

Write five dialogues matching the words of congratulation with suitable responses.

Congratulations	Responses
a. Congratulations! We wish you both a happy married life.	a. I couldn't believe my ears when the results were declared. Thanks a lot.

(Contd...

b. May I offer my congratulations on your appointment to the Board of Studies? You've done the college proud*.

c. My mother told me you had a baby girl. Congrats.

d. Hey, what's this I hear? You're the president of the students union. That was your dream, wasn't it? I'm thrilled for you.

e. It's my privilege to congratulate you on being elected as the secretary of the residents' association. You have great qualities of leadership and I'm sure you will use them fruitfully.

b. Thank you, sir. I hope I'll be able to live up to your expectations.

c. Thank you. You've been a great support to me.

d. Thanks. You must come and see her. She's such an angel.

e. Thank you for coming.

ACTIVITY 4

Enact the dialogues you have put together in activity 3 with your partner.

ACTIVITY 5

Complete the dialogues below with the expressions you have learnt in the unit. After you finish, compare your dialogues with what you will hear on CD.

a. *A*: .... on your engagement. When is the wedding?
   B: .... My parents would like to have it in May.

b. *A*: I heard the mango crop was good this season. .... I hope you'll get a good price.
   B: I hope so too. ....

* *You've done us proud* is another way of saying *We're proud of you*.

c. *A*: ....your winning the municipal elections.
   B: .... I'm grateful for the support you gave me.

d. *A*: Wow*, ...! I heard you got the job at the bank. When is the treat coming?
   B: .... I'm planning to invite you home next week for mother's delicious fish curry and rice.

e. *A*: I would like to .... the birth of a daughter. I'm sure she'll be a joy to you and your family.
   B: ....

GROUP WORK

Activity 6

Form groups of ten. Choose a partner and enact before your group one dialogue each from activity 5. Each group will thus enact all the five dialogues.

* . *Wow* is an interjection used in informal situations when you are surprised or impressed by something.

MODULE 4

UNIT 19

PAYING COMPLIMENTS, SHOWING APPRECIATION, OFFERING ENCOURAGEMENT AND RESPONDING TO THEM

One of the functions of language is to make others around us feel good about themselves by praising them, or saying something nice about them such as, for example, that somebody looks good or that he/she does something well. Responding appropriately to compliments is a part of using language well. Similarly, it helps if you are able to express the pleasure you feel when something is well done, good or useful and also to encourage others so that they feel inspired to perform better. This unit will help you learn how to do all this confidently and fluently.

भाषेचे एक कार्य आहे की आपल्या भोवतालची माणसे जेव्हा छान दिसतात, छान काम करतात तेव्हा त्यांच्याविषयी चांगले बोलून, त्यांची स्तुती करून त्यांना स्वत:विषयी चांगले वाटायला लावणे. स्तुतीला योग्य प्रकारे उत्तर देणे हा भाषेचा चांगला वापर करण्याचा एक भाग आहे. तसेच कधी काही चांगले, छान, उपयुक्त केले तर झालेला आनंद व्यक्त करता आला आणि इतरांचे कौतुक करून त्यांना अधिक चांगले काम करण्यासाठी प्रोत्साहन दिले तर त्याचा फायदा होतो. हे सारे आत्मविश्वासाने आणि अस्खलितपणे कसे करायचे हे या पाठात शिकता येईल.

a Paying compliments and responding to them

Listen carefully to the dialogues below on CD and follow them in the book. You will hear people being complimented on their appearance, clothes and talents.

Dialogue 1

(Pratima meets Sudha at a wedding. Pratima praises Sudha's appearance.)

Pratima : Sudha, **you look lovely. I like you in a** long plait with flowers in your hair.

Sudha : **Thanks,** Pratima. **You look great too. I'm glad you've** put up your hair. **The style suits you.**

Pratima : **Had to. My hair's not very thick.**

Sudha : **But you really look good with** your hair put up.

Pratima : **Thanks,** Sudha.

Dialogue 2

(Arjun sees Nikhil on his new scooter outside a bank.)

Arjun : **Wow, your** new scooter **looks good**!

Nikhil : **Thanks. I'm glad you like it.**

Arjun : **I think it's very smart. Particularly the colour**. The deep purple looks much better than the usual black.

Nikhil : **Yes, I love the colour too.**

Dialogue 3

(Surender submits a project report to his boss, who compliments him for doing the work well.)

Boss : (going through the report) **You've done a good job,** Surender. **I knew I could depend on you.**

Surender : **Thank you very much, sir. Your compliment means a lot to me.**
Boss : **I also appreciate your finishing the project on time.**
Surender : **Thank you, sir. I owe it to the training the company has given us.**
Boss : **It's nice of you to say that,** Surender.

DIALOGUE 4

(Jeevan sees a man whom he knows carrying a smart briefcase at the bus stop.)

Jeevan : **I've been admiring your briefcase. It looks so smart.**
Acquaintance : **Oh, thank you.**
Jeevan : **Would you mind telling me where you bought it? I'd like to buy one too.**
Acquaintance : These bags have been on sale at Lepakshi since Friday.
Jeevan : Thank you. I'll go there right away.

Useful points to remember

- We can compliment people on their appearance, as in *You look lovely.*
- We may refer to a particular aspect we find attractive, as in . . . *a long plait*
- We can respond to compliments with simply *Thanks/Thank you.*
- We can also respond by returning the compliment, as in *You look good too.*
- While responding to a compliment, we may sometimes want to be modest as in, *I had to (put up my hair). My hair's not very thick.*
- We can give a general compliment and follow it with a specific one, as in *Wow, that looks good. Particularly the colour.*
- We can compliment people by saying that we would like to have something they have. However, though we can ask where something was bought, it is not polite to ask its price.

Here are a few other sample compliments and responses to them.

Situation	Compliment	Response
1. At a meal	1. a. The meal was delicious, especially the laddus. You must've taken a lot of trouble over them.	1. a. Thanks. It wasn't much trouble. It's a pleasure to have you over, and anyway, I love cooking.
	b. I just love your payasam. Can I have some more?	b. Sure. That's the best compliment you can pay me. Thank you.
2. At a house-warming	2. What a beautiful house! You've planned it very well. I like the courtyard at the back.	2. Thank you. It's all because of your advice and support.
3. On seeing a baby	3. Oh, how cute she is! Such a sweet smile!	3. Thanks. Yes, she's a very friendly baby.
4. On a painting done by a friend's sister	4. That's a lovely painting! Your sister's really gifted.	4. Thanks. I'm happy you think so.

ACTIVITY 1

Listen again to dialogues 1 to 4 and repeat each line for practice.

PAIR WORK

ACTIVITY 2

Enact the sample dialogues with a partner.

ACTIVITY 3

Write responses to the compliments below, using expressions from the table. After you finish, listen to the completed exchanges on CD and enact them with your partner.

a. *Sujay* : You have beautiful handwriting. How I wish I could write like you!

Niranjan : ....

b. *Mohsin* : You've brought up your children very well, Sarita. It's a pleasure talking to them.

Sarita : ....

c. *Roy* : I'd like to compliment you on your daughter's performance. You must be proud of her.

Mrs Rajan : ....

d. *Ramesh* : Such a lovely sweater! Grey is my favourite colour. You must've slogged over it.

Kavita : ....

e. *Patient* : Doctor, I really admire your patience and commitment towards your work.

Doctor : ....

ACTIVITY 4

Write compliments to go with the following responses using any of the expressions that appear in the unit. After you finish, compare your exchanges with those that you will hear on CD and enact them with your partner.

a. *You* : Excuse me, where did you buy your kurta? ....

Stranger : Why, thanks. I bought it at Abids.

b. *Teacher* : .... at the debate. I knew you'd get a prize.

Student : Thank you, sir. It's nice of you to say so. I wouldn't have been able to do it without your help with the points.

c. *Keerti* : I like your mother's cooking, Ranjit. ....

Ranjit : Thanks. Yes, I love her chappatis too.

d. *Manoj* : Your story is .... I read it three times.

Rahul : Thanks. I'm glad you liked it so much.

e. *Director* : You played the role of Azad .... It brought tears to people's eyes.

Actor : Thank you very much for the compliment. I think it must have been all the rehearsals we did.

ACTIVITY 5

Fill in the blanks in the table. After you finish, compare your dialogues with those that you will hear on CD and enact them with your partner.

Situation	Compliment	Response
a. At the fruit stall	a. The mangoes I bought at your stall yesterday were very sweet.	a. .... Can I give you five kilos?
b. At the doctor's clinic	b. ....the way you give injections, sister. They don't hurt at all.	b. .... You're also a good patient.
c. At the Shishu Vihar nursery school	c. I think you're .... My daughter simply loves you.	c. ...., ma'am. I'm also fond of her.

b Showing appreciation

Listen carefully to the dialogues below and follow them in the book.

DIALOGUE 5

(Rekha has been helping David to work out problems in geometry.)

David : Rekha, **I can't tell you how grateful I am to you for** helping me solve these problems. **You explained them so clearly. I wouldn't have been able to understand them on my own. Thank you so very much.**

Rekha : **You're welcome**, David. It was a pleasure to work out the sums with you.

DIALOGUE 6

(Girija looks after Sashikala's children for the day.)

Sashikala : **I really appreciate your kindness** in sending lunch to school for my children. It made it possible for me to be with my mother during her surgery. **Thank you very much.**

Girija : **What are friends for,** Sashikala? **You have helped me too, haven't you**?

DIALOGUE 7

(Sagar manages to sort out a misunderstanding between two of his friends. His father appreciates him for it.)

Father : **I liked the point you made about** trying to see each other's point of view, Sagar. **Also, you spoke to them quietly when they were angry. I think it helped calm them.**

Sagar : Thanks, father. They're good friends of mine, and I can't bear to see them quarrelling.

DIALOGUE 8

(Vinod appreciates Kiran's painting.)

Vinod : (*looking at the painting of a landscape*) **That's a clever way of** drawing trees, Kiran. **I like how** you've blended different shades of green with white.

Kiran : **Thanks for appreciating** my painting, Vinod. **Your comment means so much to me because you're** an artist yourself.

Useful points to remember

- We show appreciation
  - when we are grateful for someone's help.
  - when we admire someone's abilities.
- We can show appreciation by
  - using a general expression of appreciation: *That's a clever way of . . .*
  - giving a specific reason for the appreciation: *I like how you've blended . . .*
- When someone appreciates us, we respond in the same way as when we are given a compliment, by thanking the person and suggesting how important the appreciation is to us.

ACTIVITY 6

Listen again to dialogues 5 to 8 and repeat each line for practice.

PAIR WORK

ACTIVITY 7

Enact the sample dialogues with your partner.

ACTIVITY 8

Complete the dialogues with suitable expressions of appreciation chosen from those in the box below. After you finish, listen to the CD to check your answers and enact the dialogues with your partner.

a. *Teacher* : ....the trouble you've taken to make the windmill work, Stephen.

Stephen : Thank you, sir. Your appreciation means a lot to me.

b. *Mrs Naidu* : .... if you hadn't helped me with all the arrangements for Sita's wedding.

Mrs Das : I enjoyed doing it. I think of Sita as my own daughter, don't I?

c. *Guest* : I must say that ....to spend a whole day with me at the Salar Jung museum.

Host : It was my pleasure. I enjoyed showing you the treasures of the museum.

d. *Headmistress* : Ms Mohan, ... the children speak in English to each other. That's a good way to help them use the language.

Teacher : Thank you, ma'am.

I wouldn't have managed	I'm happy you make	it was kind of you	I appreciate

C Offering encouragement

Listen carefully to the dialogues below and follow them in the book.

DIALOGUE 9

(Veena has failed a test. Amit offers her encouragement.)

Amit : **Don't lose hope,** Veena. **I'm sure you'll do better next time.**

Veena : **Thanks**, Amit. **You've given me confidence** to try again.

Dialogue 10

(Seema's coach encourages her as she practises for the Sports Day.)

Coach : **Carry on, Seema. You're doing very well.**
Seema : **Thanks for your support**, sir.

Activity 9

Listen again to dialogues 9 and 10 and repeat each line for practice.

PAIR WORK

Activity 10

Enact the sample dialogues with your partner.

Here are a few other expressions you could use

to show appreciation	to offer encouragement
1. **Great work! You've put in a lot of effort.**	1. **Don't worry. These things happen. We shouldn't lose heart.**
2. Your voice **is very good. I enjoyed your** singing.	2. **I'm here for you. Don't be disheartened.**
3. **How kind of you to** take my class! **I** feel **much better** after resting this afternoon.	3. **Well done! You can make it to the top.**
4. **What a great help you were! I liked the way you** rearranged my room.	4. **Very good! With a little more effort,** you can beat your opponent.

Activity 11

Fill in the blanks with expressions of appreciation or encouragement that you would use in the given situations. You can choose from among the expressions that appear in the unit. The first blank is filled for you as an example. After you finish, listen to the CD to check your answers.

situation	appreciation or encouragement
1. Ramesh is trying to walk after the doctor removes the cast from his fractured leg.	1. **Come on,** Ramesh! **You can do it. Don't be scared.**
2. Tara doesn't get the job she had applied for at the bank.	
3. Your mother knits a beautiful sweater for you.	
4. Your grandfather teaches you to water the rice fields.	
5. Your little sister has cleaned up her shelf on her own.	

Activity 12

Take turns with your partner to say the words of appreciation and encouragement aloud for practice.

Module 4

Unit 20 Asking for, Giving and Refusing Permission

When we ask someone for permission to do something, we ask them to allow us to do it. If we permit something, we allow it to happen or be done. In this unit, you will learn to use different expressions to politely ask for permission, and to give permission or not to give it.

आपण कोणाकडून काही करण्याची परवानगी मागतो तेव्हा आपण ती गोष्ट त्यांनी आपल्याला करू द्यावी यासाठी विचारणा करतो. आपण परवानगी देतो म्हणजे गोष्ट व्हावी, केली जावी यासाठी मान्यता देतो. सभ्यपणे परवानगी कशी मागावी, कशी द्यावी किंवा देऊ नये याचे विविध मार्ग या पाठात तुम्हाला शिकायला मिळतील.

Listen to the dialogues below and follow them in the book. The samples are set in both formal and informal situations where permission is asked for and given.

Dialogue 1 (formal)

(Sujata and her classmates are planning to put up a play in college. They ask their teacher for permission to practise their parts in the auditorium.)

Sujata : Sir, **could you permit us to** use the auditorium, **please.** We have to practise the play we're doing for Founder's Day.

Teacher : **All right**. But please see that you don't make any noise.

Sujata : **Thank you**, sir. I assure you we won't disturb anyone.

DIALOGUE 2 (FORMAL)

(Subhash would like to leave college by 12 noon because he has to participate in a painting competition at 2 p.m. He asks his principal for permission to leave.)

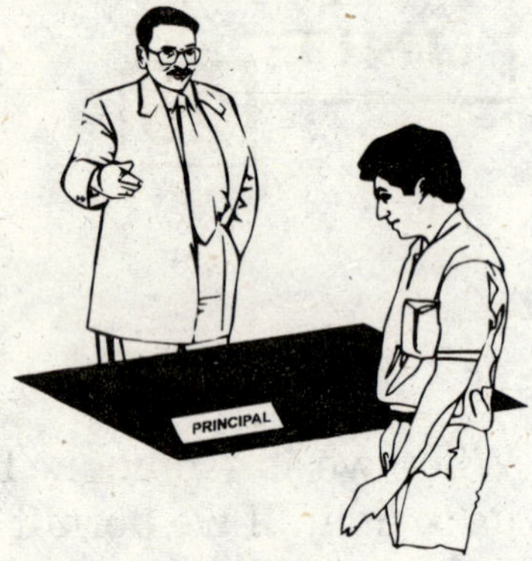

Subhash : Good morning, sir.

Principal : Good morning, Subhash. (Is) anything the matter?

Subhash : Sir, **may I** leave college early today, please. I'm participating in the inter-college painting competition, sir.

Principal : **Yes, you may**. When is the competition?

Subhash : At two in the afternoon.

Principal : Good luck.

Subhash : **Thank you**, sir.

DIALOGUE 3 (FORMAL)

(Salman Khadir has been asked to attend an interview. But he is ill, and asks for permission on phone to attend the interview at a later date. Time: 10.30 a.m. on 9th July.)

Reception : Good morning. Felextronics.

Salman : Good morning. I'm Salman Khadir. I have to appear for an interview at 10 a.m. tomorrow. But I've got the flu[20.3]. **I wonder if I could** take the interview at a later date.

Reception : Just a moment, please. I'll check with the personnel manager. (*long pause*) **That would be fine**, Mr Khadir. **You could** come for the interview at 2 p.m. on 17th July.

Salman : **Thank you very much indeed**.

Reception : You're welcome.

20.3 Note that we say *I've got* ***the flu***, but *I had* ***flu*** and *She's in bed with* ***flu***.

DIALOGUE 4 (FORMAL)

(The office bearers of the students association of a college are to have a meeting with the principal and the counsellor. Just as the meeting is about to begin, the secretary, Venktat Reddy, realises he has forgotten to get a notepad for jotting down the minutes. He asks for permission to get it. Time: 4 p.m.)

Principal : Good afternoon everyone.
Students : Good afternoon, sir.
Principal : Shall we begin?
Venkat : **Excuse me**, sir, I've forgotten to bring my notebook. **Would you mind if I got it?**
Principal : **No. Not at all.**
Venkat : Thank you, sir. I'll be back in a minute.

DIALOGUE 5 (INFORMAL)

(Dilip is in a hostel. He and his friends want to study together for an exam. Dilip does not want to disturb his room-mate and asks him for permission to study every evening from 6 to 8 p.m., when he is usually out.)

Dilip : My friends and I would like to study together for the exam. **Is it all right if** we do so from six to eight every evening?
Sudhir : **Yeah, sure**. I'll be back from basketball coaching only by half past eight.
Dilip : **Thanks a lot.**
Sudhir : **Welcome.**

DIALOGUE 6 (INFORMAL)

(Vincent has forgotten to bring his ruler. He needs it for geometry. So he asks his classmate for permission to use hers.)

Vincent : Oh dear!
Divya : What's the matter Vincent?
Vincent : I've forgotten to bring my ruler. Have you got an extra one?
Divya : Let me see (pause). Yes, I do.

Vincent : **Mind if I borrow** it for the geometry class?
Divya : **Not at all**. Here you are.
Vincent : Thanks.
Divya : **That's okay**.

Useful points to remember

✎ You can use the following expressions to ask for permission. Some of them are used only in very formal situations, while others are used only in completely informal contexts. However, most often there is no significant difference between formal and informal expressions used to ask for permission and give permission, and the same may be used in all situations. In the list below, expressions which not marked as either formal or informal can be used in all kinds of situations.

- Could I have your permission to . . .? (formal)
- We'd like your permission to . . . , please. (formal)
- Could we . . . (, please)?
- Can I . . . please? (less formal than *Could I* . . .)
- May I . . . (, please)? (formal)
- Might I/we . . .? (formal)
- I wonder if I could . . .? (formal)
- Would you mind if I . . .?
- Would you mind my . . . ing . . .?
- Do you mind if I . . .?
- Mind if I . . .? (informal)
- Would it be okay if I . . .?
- Is it all right if . . .? (informal)

✎ The following expressions are used to give permission.

- Yes, you may. (formal)
- All right.
- Of course.
- Sure.
- Yeah. Sure. (informal)
- Fine.
- Certainly. / Most certainly. (formal)
- Please do so by all means. (formal)

- Okay. (informal)
- No. Not at all. / No, of course not. (in response to the question *Would you mind if . . .?*)

- Sometimes, an expression used to give permission is supported by another expression. This is to make the person asking for permission feel that it is being given willingly.
  - Sure. Please do.
  - Sure. Why not?
  - Certainly. By all means.
- In dialogue 4, in the expression *Would you mind if . . .* , the verb form *got* is the past tense form of the verb *get*. Therefore, when you use this expression to ask for permission, you must have the past tense form of the verb you want to use. You could also say *Would you mind my getting it*?
- Sometimes you have to interrupt someone or draw his/her attention before you ask for permission. For example, in dialogue 4, Venkat draws the principal's attention (*Excuse me, sir*) before he asks for permission. You have learned how to do this politely in an earlier unit.
- In dialogue 3, the expression *I wonder if I could* . . . has a question mark at the end of the sentence because the speaker expects an answer in *Yes* (permission is given) or *No* (it is not). You would have noticed that the speaker's voice rises when asking the question. The rising tone is used not only for asking Yes-No questions but also for making requests, asking for permission, getting someone's attention or interrupting someone politely.

ACTIVITY 1

Listen again to dialogues 1 to 6 and repeat each line for practice.

PAIR WORK

ACTIVITY 2

Enact the sample dialogues with a partner.

ACTIVITY 3

In the following dialogues, fill in the blanks with some of the different expressions given above to ask for permission. After you finish, compare your dialogues with those that you will hear on CD and enact them with your partner. Remember that there is more than one acceptable answer possible.

a. *A*: .... if I turned on the television?
   B: No. Not at all.

b. *A*: ...... I borrow your chemistry book, ...?
   B: Sure.

c. *A*: I'd ....your .... to take the children to a film show on Saturday.
   B: Of course.

4. *A*: .... all right if we return the books tomorrow?
   B: All right.

ACTIVITY 4

In the following dialogues, fill in the blanks with some of the different expressions given above to give permission. After you finish, compare your dialogues with those that you will hear on CD and enact them with your partner. Remember that there is more than one acceptable answer possible.

a. *A*: I wonder if I could go to watch the cricket match on Sunday?
   B: ....

b. *A*: May I invite my friends home to tea?
   B: ....

c. *A*: Can we see the photographs you took at the rose show?
   B: ....

d. *A*: Would you mind if we took my cousins with us on the picnic?
   B: ....

GROUP WORK

ACTIVITY 5

Form groups of six. Working in pairs, write a dialogue to suit one of the following situations each. (Use your name and your friend's name(s) in the dialogue.) After everyone finishes, each pair can enact its dialogue before its group.

a. Your friends ask you if you would like to go with them to the Basar Saraswati temple.
   - You ask your parents for permission.
   - They give you permission.
   - You thank them.

b. You have to take photographs for a project report.
   - You ask your friend for permission to use his/her camera.
   - Your friend gives you permission.
   - You thank him/her.

c. You are the captain of your college cricket team and would like to watch the third test match between India and South Africa being played in Chennai the following week.
   - You ask your principal for permission to go to Chennai for a week.
   - The principal gives you permission.

Listen to the dialogues below, where permission is politely refused.

DIALOGUE 7

(Uday has to do a number of small jobs at home and he asks his boss for permission to go home early.)

Uday : Good afternoon, sir.

Boss : Good afternoon, Uday. How far have you got with the project?

Uday : I'll complete it within two days.

Boss : Please remember that our deadline is Thursday.

Uday : It'll definitely be ready by then. Sir, **could you permit me to** go home early this afternoon, **please**?

Boss : **I don't think that's a good idea**. You can't afford to take time off from the project at the moment, can you?

DIALOGUE 8

(Arvind asks the athletics coach if the team could practise during their college hours. The coach does not give the team permission to do so.)

Arvind : Good morning, sir.

Coach : Good morning Arvind. What's up?

Arvind : Sir, **may we** practise from 9.30 in the morning to 1.30 in the afternoon?

Coach : **I'd rather you didn't**. It's important for you to attend your classes. You can practise in the evening, as usual.

DIALOGUE 9

(Kavita asks her parents whether she can go trekking in the mountains with her classmates during the December holidays. Her father refuses her permission.)

Kavita : Father, my friends are going trekking in the mountains in December. **Can I go** with them?

Father : **Do you really have to?** It's going to be extremely cold, and you have just recovered from bronchitis.

DIALOGUE 10

(Mohan wants to fly kites on the hostel terrace on Sankranti. He asks the warden for permission to do so. The warden does not give him permission.)

Mohan : Good evening, sir. Tomorrow's Sankranthi. **Could we fly** kites on the terrace?

Warden : **I don't think so**. It's pretty risky.

Useful points to remember

✎ The expressions used to refuse permission are:

direct

- No, I don't think so.
- I'm sorry, but that would be difficult.
- Sorry, but I can't permit you to do that.

indirect

- I don't think that's a good idea.
- I'd rather you didn't.
- I'm sorry, but I don't see how that's possible.
- Do you really have to?

✎ When refusing permission, you can add a reason why you are doing so. For example, *I don't think so.* ***It's pretty risky***.

Activity 6

Listen again to dialogues 7 to 10 and repeat each line for practice.

PAIR WORK

Activity 7

Enact the sample dialogues with a partner.

Activity 8

Fill in the missing parts of the dialogues below using some of the expressions you have learnt to refuse permission. After you finish, compare your dialogues with those that you will hear on CD and enact them with your partner. Remember that there is more than one acceptable answer possible in each case.

a. *A*: Could I go swimming?
   B: ....

b. *A*: May we go to the midnight show?
B: …………………… .

c. *A*: Would it be okay if we go on an excursion?
B: …………………… .

d. *A*: Would you mind my putting up this poster?
B: ………………… .

GROUP WORK

ACTIVITY 9

Form groups of six. Working in pairs, write a dialogue each to suit the following situation where you are not given permission. (Each pair must write a dialogue without consulting the others). After everyone finishes, compare your dialogues with what you will hear on CD. Each pair can then enact its dialogue before the group.

- You are keen to do a part-time job.
- You apply for a job and get it.
- You ask your elder brother whether you can accept the offer.
- Your brother does not permit you to take up the job. He says it will affect your studies.

MODULE 5

UNIT 21

TALKING ABOUT THE WEATHER

We talk about the weather in different kinds of situations—when we start a casual conversation with a stranger or during one with people we know or when we specifically discuss the weather. This unit will help you learn how to talk in English about the weather. The sample dialogues here are based on the different situations in which this is done.

वेगवेगळ्या परिस्थितीत आणि वेळी आपण हवापाण्याविषयी बोलतो - अगदी परक्या व्यक्तीशी औपचारिक संभाषण सुरू करताना किंवा कधी परिचित व्यक्तींशी बोलताना किंवा कधी आपण विशेषकरून हवेविषयीच बोलत असतो. हवेविषयी इंग्लिशमधून कसे बोलायचे ते तुम्ही या पाठात शिकू शकाल. ज्या वेगवेगळ्या परिस्थितीत हे केले जाते त्यावर यातील नमुना संभाषणे आधारित आहेत.

a Talking about the weather to make small talk* with a stranger

Listen carefully to the dialogues below on CD and follow them in the book.

DIALOGUE 1

(Rajender sits next to a stranger in a bank.)

Stranger : **What a heavy downpour we had** last evening!
Rajender : **And so unexpected too, wasn't it?**

* To make small talk is to have a polite, friendly conversation about unimportant or general subjects.

Stranger : **Yes, it was really unexpected. I was completely drenched** on my way back home from the office.

Rajender : **Whoever thought it would rain so heavily?** **It was quite bright till** five o'clock. **And then, all of a sudden, black clouds darkened the sky. And before we knew it, it was pouring**[21.1].

Stranger : **And there was thunder and lightning too. I think it was a thunderstorm.** Oh, they're calling out my token number. Bye.

Rajender : Bye.

DIALOGUE 2

(Two elderly persons, Mrs Jagan and Mr Antony, sit beside each other at a music recital.)

Mrs Jagan : **It looks like it's going to be very cold this winter.**

Mr Antony : Yes, I think so too. **We're still in November, and I need a jacket in the evenings.**

Mrs Jagan : **The mist**[21.2a] **will be heavier in the mornings during December.**

Mr Antony : **I don't mind the mist so much. I love to warm myself in the mild sunlight. It's the evening chill**[21.2b] **that bothers me. That gives me a cough.** I'm glad today's the last day of the concert.

Mrs Jagan : I know[21.2c]. **I don't like coming out in this chilly weather.** Oh, look! They're starting on time today.

Mr Antony : Good.

ACTIVITY 1

Listen again to dialogues 1 and 2 and repeat each line for practice.

21.1 *It was pouring* is another way of saying *It was raining heavily.*

21.2a *Mist* is a light cloud close to the ground that makes it difficult for you to see very far.

21.2b Note that we say *evening chill* and *January chill*, but *chilly weather* and *chilly day*.

21.2c Used in spoken English to agree with someone or to tell someone that you feel the same way about something. You will learn many more ways of doing this in a later unit.

PAIR WORK

ACTIVITY 2

Enact the sample dialogues with a partner.

b Talking about the weather during a casual conversation with someone you know

Listen carefully to the dialogues below on CD and follow them in the book.

DIALOGUE 3

(Vani visits Meghana during the holidays.)

Meghana : Come in, Vani. I'm so glad you've come. **I don't like it when it keeps drizzling**[21.3a] **like this the whole day. It makes me feel sad.**

Vani : Oh, **I love the rain. I like it when it rains hard.**

Meghana : **I don't. I'm scared of thunder and lightning. I don't mind heavy rainfall during the night as long as the days are bright and sunny.**

Vani : In that case, **I wish the skies were not so overcast**[21.3b]. We could've gone to Savitri's house.

Meghana : Oh, didn't you know? Savitri's gone to her grandmother's village.

DIALOGUE 4

(Jagdish and Samson meet before the final exams.)

[21.3a] When it drizzles, it rains lightly.

[21.3b] An overcast sky is a sky made dark by clouds.

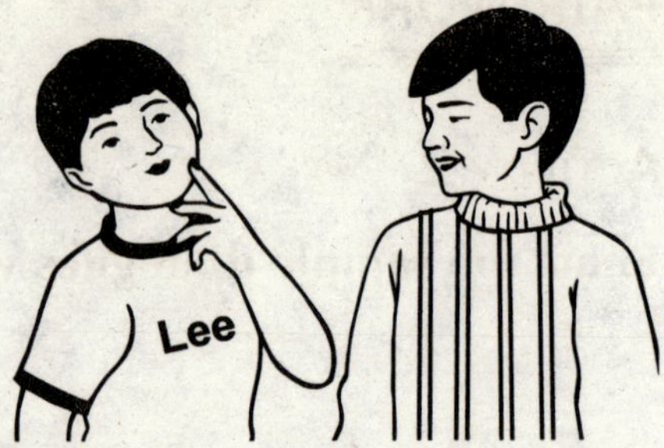

Jagdish : How's your revision going, Samson?

Samson : Not so good, Juggi. **It's hot and humid**[21.4a] **during the day.** I try to study at night.

Jagdish : **Yes, the nights are cool and breezy**[21.4b]**, aren't they?** I sit up at night too. **Wish we had a few showers to make the days cooler!**

Samson : **How can we expect rain,** Juggi? **It's just the beginning of summer right now.**

ACTIVITY 3

Listen again to dialogues 3 and 4 and repeat each line for practice.

PAIR WORK

ACTIVITY 4

Enact the sample dialogues with a partner.

C Talking specifically about the weather

Listen carefully to the dialogues below on CD and follow them in the book.

DIALOGUE 5

(Iqbal, a tourist from Kashmir, seeks Shankar's opinion on the suitability of the weather in his city for sightseeing.)

21.4a If the weather is humid, you sweat and feel hot.

21.4b If the weather is breezy, it is windy.

Iqbal : Shankar, I'll be in Hyderabad for three days and would like to see the city. D'you think May is a good time to go sightseeing?

Shankar : It would depend on whether you can stand **the summer. We have a heat wave**[21.5a] **right now. The sweltering heat**[21.5b] **will make you feel tired.** Most people **stay indoors during the day to avoid sunstroke**[21.5c]**.**

Iqbal : So you don't think being outdoors during the day will be comfortable, do you?

Shankar : **You see, the sun is scorching**[21.5d] **by** nine in the morning **and the glare can give you a headache.** Perhaps, you should visit the zoo in the morning and get to the Salar Jung museum by the afternoon **to beat the heat**[21.5e]. You could walk around the Charminar in **the cool of the evening.**

Iqbal : Thank you.

Shankar : You're welcome. Hope you have a good time.

DIALOGUE 6

(Naresh and Ramya are watching a programme on agriculture on TV.)

Naresh : It's really sad how **the unseasonable**[21.6a] **rains have destroyed the crops** this year.

Ramya : I know. My uncle in Nellore lost his entire groundnut crop because **the fields got flooded**.

Naresh : Last year was bad too for farmers. The **temperature fell to almost** ten **degrees Centigrade** in early December, resulting in a low yield.

21.5a A heat wave is a long period of unusually hot weather.

21.5b Sweltering heat is extreme, uncomfortable heat.

21.5c You have sunstroke when you have fever caused by being out in the sun for too long. Note: Do not say *a sunstroke*.

21.5d The sun is scorching when it is so strong that it burns the skin.

21.5e *To beat the heat* is to escape the heat.

21.6a Used to say that the weather is colder, hotter or more rainy than usual at a particular time of the year.

Ramya : And d'you remember what happened the year before that? **There was drought**[21.6b] in many areas of the state.

Naresh : Seems that farmers never have perfect weather on their side!

DIALOGUE 7

(Paul and Vasanta talk about the weather in distant Himachal Pradesh.)

Paul : Vasanta, you just got back from Himachal, didn't you? I heard **it's snowing**[21.7] **heavily** there.

Vasanta : Yes, that's right. **Roads, trees and houses are all covered with snow. It's a beautiful sight.**

Paul : I haven't seen snow. What does it look like?

Vasanta : Well, **it's soft, white and powdery**.

Paul : Don't you **freeze when walking in snow**?

Vasanta : Not if you're wearing enough warm clothes. It's fun actually.

ACTIVITY 5

Listen again to dialogues 5, 6 and 7 and repeat each line for practice.

PAIR WORK

ACTIVITY 6

Enact the sample dialogues with a partner.

Useful points to remember

✎ When talking to strangers about the weather, we generally agree with whatever comments they make because the purpose of the remarks is to

21.6b Drought is a long period of hot, dry weather when there is not enough water for plants and animals to stay alive.

21.7 When it snows, soft white bits of frozen water, known as *snow*, fall from the sky.

start a friendly conversation rather than to state facts correctly or express our opinion.

- We may express our likes and dislikes more freely to someone we know.
- We talk more exactly and in greater detail about the weather when it is the subject of discussion, or when we are talking about it specifically.

Activity 7

Match the words in the two columns and make new words. The first word is done for you. To check your answers, listen to the CD and take turns with your partner to repeat the words for practice.

snow	pour	**snowfall**
sun	stones	....
over	drops	....
heat	stroke	....
thunder	wave	....
down	storm	....
rain	cast	....
hail	fall	....

Activity 8

Match the following utterances to make short exchanges. After you finish, compare your exchanges with those that you will hear on CD and enact them with your partner. For e.g.:

***A*: I hear it's going to get hotter.**

***B*: Guess we'll have to stay indoors then.**

a. Nice weather, isn't it?	a. I don't. I prefer warm weather.
b. Looks like a hot, humid day.	b. **Guess we'll have to stay indoors then.**
c. Oh, I love it when it's chilly.	c. You're right. I'm sweating already.

d. How're the rains?	d. Yes, just right for a picnic.
e. **I hear it's going to get hotter.**	e. I know. You'd better wear a jacket.
f. It's pretty cold today.	f. Pretty good.

ACTIVITY 9

Fill in the blanks in the dialogue, using the expressions in the box below. After you finish, listen to the CD to check your answers and enact the dialogue with your partner.

(Satya is at a bus stop. A woman waiting for a bus strikes up a conversation with him.)

Woman : It's .... ?

Satya : Yes, and the hot air is stifling. We can hardly breathe.

Woman : It .... after Shivaratri. This kind of heat isn't good. It ....

Satya : My grandmother was saying the same thing. Oh, there's my bus.

Woman : Does it go to Prabhat Colony?

Satya : Yes, it does.

should've rained	*usually brings illnesses*
been very hot the last few days, hasn't it	

ACTIVITY 10

Change the situation in the following dialogue so as to have Mrs Rao going to a wedding in Vijayawada in summer, and rewrite it. You can use some of the words that appear in the sample dialogues. You could begin like this:

Mrs Jairam : How nice to see you, Mrs Rao! How did the wedding go?

Mrs Rao : Very well. It was terribly hot though. You can't imagine what summer in Vijayawada is like . . . .

(Mrs Jairam meets Mrs Rao at the market.)

Mrs Jairam : How nice to see you, Mrs Rao! How did the wedding go?

Mrs Rao : Very well. It was terribly cold though. You can't imagine what winter in the Nilgiris is like. The fog was so thick we could hardly see the neighbouring houses. We saw masses of white clouds float by, covering the tea estates.

Mrs Jairam : That sounds beautiful!

Mrs Rao : Yes, it's very pretty. But the nights are damp and very chilly.

Mrs Jairam : I guess you hadn't taken any warm clothes because our winters are much milder.

Mrs Rao : No, we hadn't. We didn't expect it to be so cold.

Activity 11

Enact the two dialogues in activity 10 with a partner.

Activity 12

Complete the dialogue below by filling in the blanks with suitable words taken from the box below. After you finish, compare your dialogue with what you will hear on CD and enact it with your partner.

(Mr and Mrs Abdullah discuss the date for their daughter's wedding.)

Mr Abdullah : When d'you think we could have Sajida's wedding?

Mrs Abdullah : In October, perhaps? I'd like a monsoon wedding.

Mr Abdullah : Not in October, Khamrun. We'll be .... What if we have .... for days on end? We may have a problem running around to make the wedding arrangements.

Mrs Abdullah : You're right. Last year, ... , and it didn't rain much. Though the sky .... , the weather .... But you can ....

was cool and pleasant	never tell with the monsoon rains
the monsoon was weak	right in the middle of the monsoon
was cloudy	a steady downpour

MODULE 5

UNIT 22 DESCRIBING DAILY ROUTINES

When we describe daily routines, we talk about the things that we or others do regularly or as a habit. We may have different kinds of routines depending on the things we usually do at home, in college, or at work. This unit teaches you how to talk about daily routines in English. You will find that the language used to describe routine activities in both formal and informal situations is the same.

दिनक्रमाचे वर्णन करताना आपण किंवा इतर लोक नियमितपणे किंवा सवयीने ज्या गोष्टी करत असतो त्यांविषयी बोलतो. साधारणपणे आपण ज्या गोष्टी घरी, महाविद्यालयात किंवा कामाच्या ठिकाणी करतो त्यानुसार आपला दिनक्रम वेगवेगळा असेल. इंग्लिशमधून दिनक्रमाविषयी कसे बोलायचे ते हा पाठ शिकवतो. तुमच्या लक्षात येईल की औपचारिक आणि अनौपचारिक परिस्थितीत दिनक्रमाचे वर्णन करण्यासाठी वापरलेली भाषा सारखीच आहे.

Listen carefully to the dialogues below and follow them in the book.

DIALOGUE 1

(Pradeep and Sanjana talk about their daily routines at home.)

Sanjana : Why are you late for singing practice every day, Pradeep?

Pradeep : I try really hard to come on time, Sanjana, but there're so many things I do before I come to college. Every morning, I **wake up** around seven. I **brush** my teeth, **have a bath** and **get dressed**[22.1a]. Then, I **put** my books in my bag according to the timetable. **Next,** I **have** my breakfast and **pack** my lunch. By the time I **put on my shoes and say goodbye to my mother, it's time to rush to the bus**

[22.1a] Also, *dress* meaning *put on clothes*. *Get dressed* is more commonly used in spoken English.

stop and take the 8.30 bus. If I miss it, I'm late.

Sanjana : I do almost everything you do, Pradeep. But **I pack** my books the previous evening, and **I get up** at six. That gives me more time in the mornings. **After my bath, I practise music for half an hour every day. And sometimes I even help my mother make breakfast**[22.1b]**.**

Pradeep : Perhaps I should also get my bag ready the day before and try to be up earlier than seven. Then I'm sure I can catch the 8.30 bus to college.

ACTIVITY 1

Listen to a shortened version of dialogue 1 and repeat each line for practice.

DIALOGUE 2

(Two teachers from different colleges discuss their respective routines.)

Mrs Venugopal : What is your routine like at the Modern Intermediate College?

Ms Pinto : I love the routine. **We start at** eight with an assembly. **There are** four teaching periods before lunch and three after lunch. **We have** different activities during the last hour every day.

Mrs Venugopal : That's a very good idea! I'm sure it's something the students look forward to. In our college, **we have** morning assembly **on** Mondays and Fridays. On all the other days of the week, **we begin with** yoga, meditation and physical exercises.

22.1b Note that instead of *Help someone* ***to do something***, we can say *Help someone* ***do something***, especially when speaking.

Activity 2

Listen to a shortened version of dialogue 2 and repeat each line for practice.

Dialogue 3

(Vidyadhar tells Sanat about his grandparents' routine.)

Sanat : Hey, Vidyadhar! Back from the village? Your grandparents won't know how to pass the time[22.3a] now that they are alone.

Vidyadhar : Oh, no! Not my grandparents. They **have an almost fixed routine**[22.3b] that leaves them with no time to feel lonely. Grandfather **goes** to the fields at dawn every day, and grandmother **supervises** the cooking. When grandfather **gets back** home, they **have breakfast** together and **settle down to read** the newspaper. **There is always** someone dropping in to see them. After lunch at 1 o'clock in the afternoon, they **have a short nap**[22.3c], and then they **sit** in the verandah, talking for a while. They **go for a walk** in the evening and **pick up** some fruits and vegetables on their way back. **They have** an early **dinner** and **watch TV** for about an hour. They **go to bed by** half past nine in the night.

Sanat : Wow, that's a tightly packed routine! I can see now why your grandparents don't have time to miss you.

Activity 3

Listen to a shortened version of dialogue 3 and repeat each line for practice.

22.3a When you do something to pass the time, you do it to stop feeling bored.

22.3b Like the expression *a fixed routine*, you can also have *an interesting routine*, *a boring routine* and *a daily routine*. Try to use these expressions when talking about routines in some of the activities in the unit.

22.3c A *nap* is a short sleep, especially during the day. Remember, you ***have** a nap* or ***take** a nap*.

DIALOGUE 4

(A teacher explains a change in the college schedule to a new student.)

Teacher : Good morning, boys! Remember, **we switch over to** the March schedule from next Monday.

Student : Excuse me, sir. Will you please tell me about the changed schedule? I'm new here.

Teacher : Of course, Dinesh. **You see, every year, at the beginning of summer, there's** a change in the timetable. **We don't start at** ten. Instead, **we come in at** eight and **have classes till** two thirty, with a short lunch break from twelve to twelve thirty. The athletes **come in at** seven and **train** for an hour before class.

Student : Thank you, sir.

Teacher : You're welcome.

ACTIVITY 4

Listen to a shortened version of dialogue 4 and repeat each line for practice.

Useful points to remember

- When talking about routine or habitual activities, we use verbs in the simple present tense form (ending in *s* / *es*, for e.g., *he goes* / *they go, she sleeps* / *I sleep, he plays* / *you play, she practises* / *we practise*).
- You will also need to say how often something happens as a routine. Here are a few expressions of frequency you can learn to use when talking about routines.
  - I don't *always* have breakfast at seven.
  - I *hardly* play during exams.
  - My sister *usually* sleeps a lot, but today she hasn't slept the whole afternoon.
  - We visit my grandparents *every* weekend.

- We *generally* go to my uncle's farm in summer.
- Rema goes to the library *once a week*.
- The monsoon begins by 10 June *every year* in Andhra Pradesh.
- We *often* go out in the evenings.
- He *never* sleeps before 12 midnight.

Dialogue 5

(Arati and Jacob talk about their current activities.)

Arati : Hello, Jacob. It's great meeting you. It's been a year since we left college.

Jacob : Hi, Arati. Nice seeing you too. Tell me what you're doing. Have you found a job?

Arati : No, I haven't. I'**m preparing** for the PSC examination. I'**m also doing** some voluntary service for an NGO. How about you?

Jacob : I don't want to start working until next year. My father's not been well, and so I'**m helping** him in his business. In the meantime, I'**m doing** a part-time course in journalism from the Ambedkar Open University.

Arati : That's nice. Well, good luck!

Jacob : Thanks. All the best to you too.

Activity 5

Listen to a shortened version of dialogue 5 and repeat each line for practice.

PAIR WORK

Activity 6

Enact the sample dialogues with a partner.

ACTIVITY 7

Use the expressions in the box to complete the following dialogue. After you finish, listen to the dialogue on CD and enact it with your partner.

(Govind tells his mother about his baby.)

Mother : So, how's little Ranji doing?

Govind : She's such an angel. She .... most of the time.

Mother : Does she sleep during the day? She should, you know.

Govind : Oh, yes, she does. She .... after lunch.

Mother : What does she like to eat?

Govind : She .... boiled potatoes and curd.

Mother : When does she have a bath?

Govind : Veena or I .... in the afternoon.

Mother : I'm so glad she's coming on well. God bless her.

loves	sleeps for an hour	plays by herself	give her a bath

GROUP WORK

ACTIVITY 8

Form groups of three. The table below has information on how Premila, Tony and Salma spent their holidays last summer. Imagine that they follow the same routine again this summer and fill in the blanks in one of the routines each. After you finish, compare your descriptions with those that you will hear on CD and tell the others in your group about the routine you completed.

Premila	Tony	Salma
6 a.m. – 7 a.m. practised music	6 a.m. – 7 a.m. yoga class	6 a.m. went for a walk
9 a.m. – 10 a.m cooked lunch	9 a.m. – 10 a.m helped father in his shop	9 a.m. – 10 a.m cleaned the house
4 p.m. – 5 p.m. played basketball	4 p.m. – 5 p.m. watched TV	2 p.m. – 3 p.m. took a nap
5 p.m. – 6 p.m. worked in the garden	5 p.m. – 6 p.m. went swimming	6 p.m. – 8 p.m. studied
6 p.m. – 7 p.m. went for Hindi tuition	6 p.m. – 7 p.m. took the dog out	8 p.m. – 9 p.m. played chess with brother
8 p.m. – 10 p.m. spent time with the family	8 p.m. – 9 p.m. read	9.30 p.m had dinner
10.30 p.m. went to bed	9.30 p.m. went to bed	10 p.m. – 11 p.m. listened to music
		11 p.m. went to bed

a. Premila .... between six and eight in the morning every day. She .... between 9 a.m. and 10 a.m. In the evening, between five and six, Premila .... She .... between six and seven. Later, she .... two hours with her family. Premila .... at 10.30 p.m.

b. Tony ....for yoga class between six and seven in the morning. He ....his father in his shop from 9 a.m. to 10 a.m. Between four and seven in the evening, Tony .... , ... and .... He .... for an hour from eight to nine every night. Tony .... to bed at half past nine.

c. Salma .... at six in the morning every day. She .... the house from nine to ten. After lunch, she .... a nap between two and three in the afternoon. Salma .... from six in the evening for two hours. She .... chess every day for an hour with her brother. Salma .... dinner at half past nine. She .... to music for an hour from ten at night and .... to bed at eleven.

MODULE 5

UNIT 23 TALKING ABOUT POSSESSIONS

When we refer to possessions, we mean all those things we own or have with us at a given time. People who are related to us in some way, such as our family and friends, belong to us too. The word 'possessions' can also refer to territories which are occupied by another country. In this unit, we shall learn words and expressions to talk about our possessions.

मालमत्तेचा निर्देश करताना आपण आपल्या मालकीच्या किंवा एका विवक्षित वेळी आपल्याजवळ असलेल्या साऱ्या गोष्टी गृहीत धरलेल्या असतात.आपल्याशी काही संबंध असलेल्या व्यक्ती म्हणजे आपले कुटुंब आणि मित्र हेही ''आपले'' असतात. ''मालकीचे असणे'' याचा संदर्भ दुसऱ्या देशाच्या ताब्यातील प्रदेश असाही जोडता येतो. या पाठात आपण आपल्या मालकीच्या वस्तूंविषयी बोलताना वापरावयाची भाषा शिकणार आहोत.

Listen carefully to the dialogues below on CD and follow them in the book.

DIALOGUE 1

(Radha finds a purse on the badminton court after her classmates have gone to their classroom. She picks it up and goes there to find out who the owner is.)

Radha : Excuse me, everyone. **Whose** purse is this?

Lalit : Oh, that's **mine**. Thank you so much. It must have fallen out of **my** pocket.

Radha : I hope you haven't lost anything. Please check.

Lalit : (*opens the purse*). Ah! Thank god, **my** locket's in here. It's very precious. **My** grandmother gave it to me.

Radha : And what about the other things?

Lalit : Let me see. (*pause*) Yes, I **have my** money and **my** ATM card too. Everything's there.

DIALOGUE 2

(Chetan asks his friend Pavan to guess what Asif has in his bag.)

Chetan : Can you guess what Asif **has got** in that bag?

Pavan : Hmm . . . **His** tracksuit?

Chetan : No. It's a small cricket bat with Tendulkar**'s** autograph.

Pavan : **Whose** is it?

Chetan : Karan**'s** and Ravi**'s.**

Pavan : Is it really **theirs**? I can't believe it.

Chetan : Yes. They got **his** autograph on the last day of the test match.

DIALOGUE 3

(Kapil, Shilpa and Sreenath talk about their most precious possessions during lunch break.)

Kapil : Shilpa, of all the things you possess, what's most precious to you?

Shilpa : Well, **my** black beads. I always wear them round my neck. **My** mother gave them to me. What's **yours** Kapil?

Kapil : I **have** quite a few possessions that are very precious. But the one that's most precious is a small wooden aeroplane that I carved with a pen knife when I was six. And you, Sreenath?

Sreenath : **My** most precious possession is a bunch of roses made of glass. **My** sister gave it to me on my tenth birthday.

DIALOGUE 4

(Anand and his classmates are at an NCC camp. It is the last day of training. An officer asks them to check all their belongings.)

Officer : Please pack **your** bags and make sure you don't leave any of **your** belongings[23.4] behind.

Anand : Yes, sir. Where're **our** mugs? *(looks around)* Are these mugs **ours**?

Officer : Yes, they're **yours**. Each of you can take one. Put them in **your** kit bags.

Anand : We will, sir.

DIALOGUE 5

(A teacher wants to return her students' belongings that they had brought to college for an exhibition.)

Teacher : Anita, is this Ravi's chart?

Anita : No, ma'am. It's **mine**.

Teacher : Isn't this model Shweta's?

Anita : Yes, ma'am. It's **hers**.

Teacher : Which of these staplers is Sanjay's?

Anita : *(pointing to a plastic stapler)* That's **his**.

Teacher : Are these boxes Vasu's and Fasiha's?

Anita : No, ma'am, not these. *(pointing to two boxes in a corner)* Those are **theirs**.

Teacher : Isn't this **your** candle, Anita?

Anita : No, ma'am. **Mine** is not so big. This is **yours**.

Useful points to remember

✎ To say that we possess something, we use *have (got) / has (got)*. Say, for example:

- I **have** a pet.
- We **have** a pet.

23.4 another word for *possessions*

- You **have** a pet.
- They **have** a pet.

but He / she **has** a pet.

- It **has** long ears.

Note that when speaking, we do not use the shortened forms *I've, we've, you've, he's, she's, it's* and *they've* to talk about possessions, as we would when we say, for example, in ***I've** washed the shirt* or ***She's** gone to Mahbubnagar.* However, we use the shortened forms when *have* is followed by *got,* as in *I've got a new bicycle* and *She's got a red umbrella.*

To say that we possess something, we also say that it *belongs* to us.

✎ To find out whom something belongs to, we usually ask the question *Whose . . . is this / are these?*

✎ Another way of asking the same question is *To whom does / do ...... belong?*

✎ To talk about possessions we use the pronouns *my, our, your, his/her* and *their*, before the word for the thing we possess. For example:

- **My** pen is not working.
- **Our** books are at the bottom of the pile.
- He borrowed **your** dictionary.
- Kamala found **her** sunglasses in the car.

- This is **his** house.
- Look at the new car. This is **its** steering wheel.
- **Their** passports are with the travel agent.

✎ We can also talk about possessions, using sentences where the pronoun comes at the end. For example:

- The pen that's not working is **mine.**
- The books at the bottom of the pile are **ours**.
- The dictionary he borrowed was **yours**.
- The sunglasses Kamala found in the car were **hers**.
- This house is **his**.
- The passports with the travel agent are **theirs**.

Note that there is no change in the form of the pronoun *his*. Also note that we do not say *The steering wheel is* ***its***.

✎ When we write, we do not use an apostrophe (') in the words *ours, yours, hers, its and theirs*, as we do with personal names, such as *Fasiha's*.

Activity 1

Listen again to dialogues 1–5 and repeat each line for practice.

PAIR WORK

Activity 2

Enact the sample dialogues with a partner.

Activity 3

Fill in the blanks in the following dialogues, choosing a suitable word from those given in brackets. After you finish, compare your dialogues with those on CD and enact them with your partner.

a. *A*: .... (which /whose) cards are these?
   B: These are ....(my /mine) cards.

b. *A*: These are some of .... (his's / his) favourite things.
   B: Aren't they .... (your / yours) favourite things?
   A: Yes, they're .... (my / mine) too.

c. *A*: .... (our / ours) paintings aren't as colourful as .... (their / theirs).
   B: Yes, ... (their / theirs) paintings are certainly more beautiful than .... (our / ours).

d. *A*: To ...... (whose / whom) does this pen belong?
   B: It's not .... (my / mine).

e. *A*: Are these pencils .... (her / hers)?
   B: Yes. They're .... (her / hers) pencils.

f. *A*: .... (I have / I've) an old bicycle that I won't part with.
   B: Why not?
   A: Because .... (its / it's) won me several races.

GROUP WORK

ACTIVITY 4

Form groups of six and fill in the blanks in the dialogues below with suitable expressions that indicate possessions. Compare your dialogues with those that you will hear on CD. Each member of a group can then enact one of the dialogues with a partner.

a. *Karuna* : Where's .... bag?
Satish : Which one? I .... got three of them.
Karuna : I'm not sure which ones you ....
Satish : Well, ... new one is blue and red.
Karuna : Ah yes! That's the one I meant.

b. *Sharat* : Could I borrow .... crayons please?
Sreevani : I'm sorry. I don't .... any.
Sharat : .... are these on your desk?
Sreevani : They aren't .... They're ...., Shraddha's.
Sharat : Excuse me, Shraddha are these .... ?
Shraddha : Yes.
Sharat : Can I borrow them, please?
Shraddha : Of course.
Sharat : Thanks.

c. *Benny* : Look at the beautiful potted plants in Uma's garden!
Leela : Do they all belong to ....?
Benny : No, only the ones near the gate are ....
Leela : What about the plants on the verandah? .... are those?
Benny : They are .... sister, Suma's. Uma's taking care of them until Suma comes back from Kakinada.

ACTIVITY 5

Take turns to tell the other members in your group about a possession that is very dear to you. Each of you will:

- ◈ say what the possession is.
- ◈ describe it in a sentence.
- ◈ say why you treasure it.

You could use the outline below.

> I have a / I've got a .... It is .... It is dear to me because .... father/ mother/ grandmother / grandfather / uncle/ aunt / friend gave it to me the year I passed my class 10 exam.

MODULE 5

UNIT 24

TALKING ABOUT CURRENT ACTIVITIES

When we describe current activities, we talk either about activities that are being done and that have not come to an end or about activities that are being done regularly (every day or often at intervals) during a period of time that includes the time of speaking. Thus, for example, imagine that you have just sat down to write a story. If someone asks you what you are doing, you will say *I'm writing a story.* On the other hand, if you have been regularly spending all your free time during the past one month writing a story little by little, your reply to the question would again be *I'm writing a story.* This unit will help you learn how to describe current activities and events.

चालू कामकाजाचे वर्णन करताना आपण बोलत असलेल्या कालावधीत चालू असलेल्या, अजून न संपलेल्या कामाविषयी किंवा नियमितपणे (दररोज किंवा बऱ्याचदा थोड्या थोड्या वेळाने) केल्या जाणाऱ्या कामांविषयी बोलतो. म्हणजे समजा तुम्ही आताच एक गोष्ट लिहीण्यासाठी बसला आहात. कोणी तुम्हाला विचारले की तुम्ही काय करत आहात तर तुम्ही सांगाल **मी गोष्ट लिहीत आहे**. दुसरीकडे, तुम्ही गेला महिनाभर तुमचा मोकळा वेळ खर्च करून नियमितपणे थोडी थोडी गोष्ट लिहीत असाल तर त्या प्रश्नाला तुमचे उत्तर परत तेच असेल की **मी गोष्ट लिहीत आहे**. चालू घडामोडी आणि घटना यांचे वर्णन करावयाला तुम्हाला हा पाठ शिकवतो.

Listen carefully to the dialogues below on CD and follow them in the book.

DIALOGUE 1

(Shanta is watching a film with her 5-year-old son.)

Shanta : Hari, tell me what the man in the dhoti is doing?
Hari : He'**s digging** a hole in the ground.

Shanta : What's he doing now? Has he finished digging the hole?

Hari : Yes, he has dug a deep hole. He**'s putting** a coconut sapling in the hole.

Shanta : And now?

Hari : He**'s covering** its roots with soil.

Shanta : Has he finished?

Hari : Yes. The man**'s watering** the sapling now.

DIALOGUE 2

(Kalpana speaks to her brother on the telephone.)

Kalpana : Hello. Kalpana here.

Vikas : Hi. Where are you? You're late today and we're all worried.

Kalpana : I'm sorry. I'm still in office. We have an important meeting at six. What's everyone doing?

Vikas : Well, mother**'s reading** the newspaper and **glancing**[24.2] at the clock every five minutes. Father**'s walking** up and down the street, **waiting** to see if you're coming. Grandfather**'s watching** TV, and Kiran**'s studying** for her physics test.

Kalpana : And you?

Vikas : I**'m listening** to music.

Kalpana : Okay. Tell mother that Meena will drop me back home after the meeting, will you?

Vikas : Fine.

[24.2] To glance is to quickly look at someone or something.

DIALOGUE 3

(Sachin tells his neighbour about what he has been doing.)

Shobha : Good morning, Sachin! I haven't seen you in ages. Where have you been?

Sachin : I've been busy, Shobha. We**'re preparing** for the Independence Day celebrations at college.

Shobha : Oh, really? That sounds interesting.

Sachin : The NCC cadets **are practising for** the march-past. Some of us **are learning** patriotic songs. The seniors **are enacting** the First War of Independence in a dance drama. We**'re planning** a grand programme this year.

Shobha : Do you think I could come to watch it?

Sachin : Sure. You're welcome.

DIALOGUE 4

(Veena explains why she has to miss the holiday trip her friends wanted her to join.)

Veena : I'm sorry I won't be able to go to Vizag with you, Annie. You see I**'m taking care** of my little niece.

Annie : Why, isn't your sister home?

Veena : No, she's in hospital for minor surgery[24.4]. I**'m** also **cooking and cleaning** as everyone's at the hospital most of the time.

Annie : Never mind. You can join us next time.

DIALOGUE 5

(Mr Khan talks to his wife about visiting their friends.)

Mr Khan : Fatima, how about visiting the Raos this evening?

Mrs Khan : That would've been nice, but Vijay **is working** late today. I spoke to Shama this morning.

[24.4] Do not say *a minor surgery*.

Mr Khan : But he has a five-day week[24.5], doesn't he?

Mrs Khan : Yes, he does. But he**'s going** to work every Saturday this month as he has to complete a project by the 31st.

Mr Khan : Okay. Let's make it another day then.

ACTIVITY 1

Listen again to dialogues 1–5 on CD and repeat each line for practice.

PAIR WORK

ACTIVITY 2

Enact the sample dialogues with a partner.

Useful points to remember

- Use verbs in the form *eats, sleeps, talks*, etc., to talk about what happens usually or as a regular routine. You have learned to use this form to describe routines. For e.g.:
  - Lekha's mother *plays* the veena beautifully.
  - My uncle *works* in Mumbai.
  - We *do* all our shopping at Koti.
- Use the form *is/are/am + verb-ing* to talk about
  - an activity that has not come to an end when we are talking about it.
  - a temporary arrangement.

  For e.g.: She*'s preparing* to take the EAMCET examination.
  - I*'m cooking* lunch this week.
  - Vijay*'s working* late today.
- Do not use the *–ing* form to talk about states of mind, emotions and feelings. Thus, we do not say *I'm having a headache* for *I have a headache, She's liking milk* for *She likes milk* or *I'm understanding what you say* for *I understand what you say.*

[24.5] When you have a five-day week, you work from Monday to Friday.

ACTIVITY 3

Fill in the blanks in the dialogue below with the groups of words in the box below. After you finish, listen to the CD to check your answers and enact the dialogue with your partner, taking turns to play the two roles.

(The phone rings. Susheela answers the call.)

Susheela : Hello? Oh, Keerti! What's up?

Keerti : Hi, Sushi! Just thought I'd say hello. What're you doing?

Susheela : I .... for a test.

Keerti : What're Nita and Naveen doing?

Susheela : They .... TV. You know how crazy they are about *antakshari*.

Keerti : Yes I do. Are your parents at home?

Susheela : Yes, they .... to each other while my mother .... a new shirt for Varun. He .... in the garden.

is playing	am studying	are talking	is stitching	are watching

ACTIVITY 4

Fill in the blanks in the sentences below with the *–ing* forms of the verbs in brackets.

a. I .... of the refreshments. (take care)
b. We .... the rooms cleaned every day. (get)
c. She .... the visitors round the exhibition. (escort)
d. He .... the experiments. (explain)
e. They .... the announcements. (make)

ACTIVITY 5

Fill in the blanks in the dialogue below with the sentences you completed. After you finish, listen to the CD to check your answers and then enact the dialogue with your partner.

Teacher : I hope the science exhibition is going well. Let me check what everyone's doing. You, Rakesh?

Rakesh : Ma'am, ... the refreshments.

Teacher : Okay. What are Shruti and Asha doing?

Rakesh : Ma'am, ... the announcements.

Teacher : And George?

Rakesh : .... the experiments.

Teacher : Good. How about Yamuna?

Rakesh : .... the visitors round the exhibition.

Teacher : And, Maria, how're you and Smita helping?

Maria : .... the rooms cleaned every day, ma'am.

Teacher : Great. I'm so proud of all of you!

ACTIVITY 6

Complete the dialogue below with the appropriate forms of the verbs in brackets. The first blank has been filled for you. After you finish, listen to the CD to check your answers and enact the dialogue with your partner.

Nitish : Hello, John, it's been two years since we met. What're you doing these days? (do)

John : ....(make) documentary films now. What about you?

Nitish : .... (teach) English at a school, but ....(look) for a change.

John : Why don't you talk to Ashok? .... (plan) to start an advertising company, and I'm sure he needs people with good language skills.

Nitish : Thanks. I'll do that.

MODULE 5

UNIT 25

ASKING FOR THE TIME AND DATE

We often ask for the time and date of any event that is to take place, or of any activity we have to participate in. We ask for times and/or dates when we make inquiries about the arrivals and departures of flights, trains and buses or when we make appointments. Sometimes we also need to ask others what the time of the day or the date is.

पुढे होणाऱ्या घटनेची किंवा आपण भाग घेत असलेल्या कार्यक्रमाची तारीख आणि वेळ आपण खूप वेळा विचारतो. विमाने, रेल्वेगाड्या, बस यांच्या येण्याजाण्याच्या तसेच ठरविलेल्या भेटीच्या बाबत चौकशी करताना आपण बऱ्याचदा वेळा आणि तारखा विचारतो. कधीकधी आपल्याला इतरांना आज काय तारीख आहे किंवा आता काय वेळ आहे हे विचारावे लागते.

Listen carefully to the dialogues below and follow them in the book.

DIALOGUE 1

(Bharat calls Sneha.)

Bharat : Hello, Sneha.

Sneha : Hi, Bharat.

Bharat : I called to remind you about my brother's wedding. You must come.

Sneha : Sure. Hey, I seem to have misplaced the invitation card. The wedding's **on Friday**, isn't it?

Bharat : Yes, you're right. It's **at six o'clock in the evening on 11th June**.
Sneha : I'll certainly come.
Bharat : Bye!
Sneha : Bye, bye!

Dialogue 2

(Shravan tells his colleague about an office meeting.)

Shravan : Hi, Vasudha. I heard that you were unwell. Hope you feel better today.
Vasudha : Hi. I'm fine. Thanks.
Shravan : I wanted to tell you that the director of Omega Projects has agreed to a meeting.
Vasudha : Good. **When is it scheduled**[25.2]**, please**?
Shravan : It's **at half past three in the evening on Wednesday, the** 21st.
Vasudha : Let me make a note of it in my planner.

Dialogue 3

(Surya and Sebastian plan to meet to discuss a company project.)

Surya : Shall we have a meeting next week?
Sebastian : Yes. That's a good idea.
Surya : **What day**? Would next Wednesday suit you?
Sebastian : Let me check. Hmm . . . yes, that'd be fine.
Surya : **What time**?
Sebastian : **Ten o'clock in the morning** should be okay.

25.2 We say that something is scheduled when it is planned to happen at a particular time. Thus, we can say, for example, *The show was scheduled for 6 October, but it was cancelled because of bad weather*.

Surya : Right then. We'll meet **at 10 o'clock on Wednesday** in my room. Please try and be **on time**[25.3] because I have to catch the **12 noon** train to Lucknow.

DIALOGUE 4

(Shaurya invites Sheila to a music concert.)

Shaurya : I'm going to buy tickets for the concert on Friday. Would you like to come?

Shiela : I'd love to, thanks. **What time does the** concert **start**?

Shaurya : **At** 6.30 **in the evening**. Please be **on time**. I don't like going in late.

Shiela : Don't worry. I'll be there **by 6.15**.

DIALOGUE 5

(Harsha is at a tourist office, making inquiries.)

Harsha : **What time** does your bus leave for Film City?

Employee : **At seven in the morning.**

Harsha : **How long does it take** to get there?

Employee : **About two hours.**

Harsha : D'you have a bus service every day?

Employee : No. We have trips only **on Mondays, Wednesdays and Fridays.**

Harsha : **When will we be back?**

Employee : We'll drop you outside the Hotel Raj **between a quarter to seven and seven.**

[25.3] The expression *on time* in dialogues 3 and 4 means *at exactly the correct time* or *the time that was arranged*. This is different from the expression *in time*, which means *before time*, or *with enough time to be able to do something*. For example, *We'll definitely be* **in time** *for the 8 o'clock bus*.

Dialogue 6

(Mukund is at a bus stop. His watch has stopped working, and he needs to find out what the time is.)

Mukund (to a boy waiting for a bus)	:	Excuse me. **What time is it, please?**
Boy	:	**It's a quarter past three.**
Mukund	:	Thank you.
Boy	:	You're welcome.

Activity 1

Listen again to dialogues 1–6 and repeat each line for practice.

PAIR WORK

Activity 2

Enact the sample dialogues with a partner.

Useful points to remember

✎ Some common ways of asking the time and date of events or asking what the time of the day is and responding to such inquiries are given below.

questions	responses
- When is it?	On .... at ....
- What time?	At ..... sharp.
- When should I be there?	On the ....st at ....
- What's the time?	.... o'clock.
- What time does the. . . start?	At ..... in the .... (morning/afternoon/evening)

✎ Notice that *at* is used for points of time, that is, for the exact time and *on* is used for days and dates. For example, *at six o'clock, on Wednesday, on 11th June.*

✎ To ask what the time of the day is, we use the question *What time is it?* It is polite to say *Excuse me* before asking for the time of the day, especially if you are speaking to a stranger or trying to get someone's attention. Other ways of doing this are:

- *Could you tell me the time, please?*
- *Could you tell me what time it is, please?*
- *I'd like to know the time, please.*

✎ To ask about a period of time, we usually use *how long* + *do/does/will* + *take/last*. For example, *How long does it take to get there?* The responses to this kind of question could be exact, as in *two hours,* or approximate, as in *about forty-five minutes.*

ACTIVITY 3

Fill in the blanks in the following dialogues with suitable expressions to ask about the time of events. After you finish, listen to the CD to check your answers and enact the dialogues with your partner.

a. *A*: We came home rather late last night.
B: ………….. did the film get over?
A: At midnight.

b. *A*: I'm going to a magic show tomorrow. Would you like to come?
B: I'd love to. Thanks. …………………… the show start?
A: At 6.30 in the evening.

c. *A*: We're going to the exhibition this evening. Can you meet us there?
B: Yes. ……….. reach there?
A: At 5.00 in the evening.

d. *A*: You must attend the meeting.
B: ………. is it?
A: It's scheduled for 21st August at 10 o'clock in the morning.

ACTIVITY 4

Fill in the blanks in the following dialogues with responses to the questions about the time of events. Compare your dialogues with those you will hear on CD and enact them with your partner.

a. *A*: When does the play start?
   B: .... 4 o'clock. Please be .... time.

b. *A*: Let's practise for the football match.
   B: When d'you want to do it?
   A: .... Tuesday .... five in the evening.

c. *A*: What time does the flight from Kolkata arrive?
   B: .... 8 o'clock.

d. *A*: Can you help me move house*?
   B: Certainly. When should I be there?
   A: ....

ACTIVITY 5

Fill in the blanks in the following dialogues with suitable expressions to ask for the time and date. After you finish, compare your dialogues with those that you will hear on CD and enact them with your partner.

a. *A*: Is your meeting over?
   B: No. We didn't have a meeting at all.
   A: What a waste of time! .... to be held?
   B: At 9 o'clock.

b. *A*: Could .... the Goa Express leaves for Mumbai?
   B: At 2:40 in the afternoon, sir.
   A: .... it take to get there?
   B: About fifteen hours.

---

* The expression means to go to live in another house.

c. *A*: It's nearly 4 o'clock. But the theatre's almost empty, and the film hasn't started yet.
   B: .... to start?
   A: At 3.30 in the afternoon.

d. *A*: We did an interesting play on Republic Day.
   B: .... the play?
   A: About an hour and a half.

e. *A*: The rain has spoilt our programme.
   B: .... start raining?
   A: An hour ago. I do hope it stops soon.

GROUP WORK

ACTIVITY 6

Form groups of six. Each member of a group must ask a question about the time, date or duration of two events from the list below. The other members of the group will take turns to respond to the inquiries. Use the expressions that appear in this unit.

a. the date and time of a quiz contest
b. the time and duration of a movie
c. the date of the opening of a new shopping mall
d. the time of a dance recital that didn't take place as scheduled
e. the time of visit to a zoo
f. the time of arrival of a train
g. the duration of a bus journey to Bangalore
h. the time and date of a peace march
i. the time and date of an appointment at the dentist's
j. the time when a programme started and ended
k. the time it takes to go from a group member's home to the college
l. the time and date when a play will be staged next

Appendix A

Distinguishing between Spelling and Sound

Activity 1

a. i. Look at the following words and listen to them on the CD.

cast	called	sale	band	woman	village	what

Which letter of the alphabet is common to all the words? Does that letter 'sound' the same in all the words? Listen to the words again to find out.

You will notice that there is no one-to-one correspondence between the letter 'a' and what it 'sounds' like when the words are said aloud.

ii. Look at the following words and listen to them on the CD.

though	through	thorough	cough
rough	bough	bought	

Which letters of the alphabet are common to all the words? Do these letters represent the same sound in all the words? Listen to the words again to find out.

It is clear from the words in (i) and (ii) that the same letter of the alphabet can stand for different sounds.

b. i. Look at the following words and listen to them on the CD.

song scent descend brass assume cement
fancy pace exercise tax psychology

The words have one common consonant sound. Which letter/s stand/s for that sound in each word?

ii. Listen to some more words that have a common vowel sound.

bead weep seize believe piece theme
people key police ski quay aesthetic

The vowel sound in the word 'bee' is common to all the words. Which letters in each word represent the sound?

c. Listen to the following sets of words on the CD.

i.	question, quiet, square, squash
ii.	excuse, excite, box, exercise
iii.	exact, examine, exist, exert
iv.	unit, use (n.) utilise, university

In each set of words one of the letters represents a combination of two sounds. Listen to each set again and identify the letter.

From (a), (b) and (c) you must have noticed that it is difficult for us to know how a word is pronounced by looking at its spelling.

In (a) you saw that the same letter can stand for different sounds.

In (b) you have examples of the same sound being represented by different letters or combinations of letters.

In (c) one letter of the alphabet stands for a combination of two sounds. Thus:

q → /kw/

x → /ks/

x → /gz/

u → /ju/ (the first consonant sound in 'yes' and the vowel sound in 'cool').

To understand the difference between spelling and sound, complete the following tasks with a partner.

PAIR WORK

TASK 1

a. In the following pairs of words, tick those that are pronounced alike.

sail – sale	quite – quiet	rain – reign	weather – whether
rough – cough	heard – herd	wrap – rap	suite – sweet
piece – peace	pane – pain		

Now listen to the CD to check your answers.

b. Make a list of pairs of words (other than the ones above) that are spelt differently but pronounced alike.

TASK 2

Look at the following words and listen to them on the CD. Write down the number of letters and the number of sounds each word has. Follow the example given below.

word	*number of letters*	*number of sounds*
shelf	5	4

(a) curry (b) sign (c) box (d) common
(e) live (f) pretty (g) exact (h) bead
(i) quick (j) wrong (k) kitchen (l) college
(m) friend (n) funny (o) bridge

Check your answers with those given in the appendix at the end of the module.

TASK 3

Fill in the blanks with words that are pronounced the same as each of those given below.

(a) write .... (b) straight .... (c) mite ....
(d) sun .... (e) bow (verb) .... (f) bear ....

(g) tail .... (h) cast .... (i) sight ....
(j) roll ....

Check your answers with those given in the appendix.

TASK 4

Listen to the following words and underline the letters that are not pronounced, or that are silent.

(a) knight	(b) calm	(c) comb	(d) adjective	(e) adjust
(f) resign	(g) gnat	(h) walk	(i) column	(j) solemn
(k) folk	(l) pneumonia	(m) castle	(n) almond	(o) listen
(p) whole	(q) whose	(r) wrist	(s) doubt	(t) receipt

From the tasks you have just completed you must have noticed that the letters of the alphabet (which are twenty-six in number) are not enough to represent the forty-four sounds (vowels and consonants) that there are in English. There cannot, in other words, be a one-to-one correspondence between the alphabet and the sounds of English. To get over this problem, therefore a special set of symbols has been devised and is used in English dictionaries to indicate the pronunciation of words. Each of these symbols represents a single sound. In the next two units, you will learn the value of the symbols, that is, the sounds they stand for.

APPENDIX B

THE CONSONANTS OF ENGLISH

The phonetic symbols used for the consonant sounds of English are the same in different books and dictionaries, but the symbols used for the vowel sounds may differ slightly. The symbols given in this unit and the next are those used in the *Oxford Advanced Learner's Dictionary of Current English* (7th edition).

The symbols for the consonants of English along with key words that illustrate the sounds are given below.

ACTIVITY

Look at each symbol in the list below, listen to the sound it represents and repeat the key words.

s.no.	phonetic symbol	key words
a.	/p/	pin, spin, sip
b.	/b/	bus, tubs, rub
c.	/t/	tap, stop, hut
d.	/d/	day, body, head
e.	/k/	keys, sky, ache
f.	/g/	go, ugly, dog
g.	/tʃ/	chain, kitchen, match
h.	/dʒ/	jam, plunged, bridge
i.	/m/	move, small, come
j.	/n/	knot, snake, bin
k.	/ŋ/	brings, sing, ring

l.	/f/	fan, sphere, calf
m.	/v/	vein, shelves, sleeve
n.	/θ/	think, months, earth
o.	/ð/	that, bathes, soothe
p.	/s/	soul, caste, press
q.	/z/	zoo, noisy, breeze
r.	/ʃ/	ship, ration, brush
s.	/ʒ/	vision, treasure, rouge
t.	/h/	heat, behave, behind
u.	/l/	late, allow, sale
v.	/r/*	rate, arrest, shrink
w.	/j/	yoke, you, beyond
x.	/w/	word, watch, twist

You must have noticed that seventeen of the twenty-four symbols are familiar letters. Only seven of them are unfamiliar and need to be learnt. These are: /tʃ/, /dʒ/, /ŋ/, /θ/, /ð/, /ʃ/ and /ʒ/. Remember that the symbol /j/ stands for the first sound in the word 'you' and not for the first sound in the word 'joke'.

Listen to the consonant sounds on the CD once again before you attempt the following tasks.

PAIR WORK

TASK 1

Listen on the CD to sequences of a consonant sound followed by the vowel sound /ɑ:/ (as in the word 'last'). Identify the consonant sound in each sequence and write down the symbol representing it. For example, /bɑ:/, /kɑ:/. To check your answers, refer to the appendix at the end of the module.

* In British English, the letter 'r' is not pronounced, or it is silent, before consonant sounds. For e.g., 'worse' is pronounced /wɜ:s/. It is also not pronounced in the final position in words, as in 'car' /kɑ:/, and 'hear' /hɪə/. The letter is pronounced when it is followed by a vowel, as in 'arrest' /ərest/, 'rate' /reɪt/, 'far away' /fɑ:rəweɪ/.

(a) __ ɑː	(b) __ ɑː	(c) __ ɑː	(d) __ ɑː	(e) __ ɑː	(f) __ ɑː	(g) __ ɑː
(h) __ ɑː	(i) __ ɑː	(j) __ ɑː	(k) __ ɑː	(l) __ ɑː	(m) __ ɑː	(n) __ ɑː
(o) __ ɑː	(p) __ ɑː	(q) __ ɑː	(r) __ ɑː	(s) __ ɑː	(t) __ ɑː	(u) __ ɑː

Task 2

Listen to the words on the CD and fill in the blank spaces below with the symbols for the consonants you hear at the beginning and the end of each of them. Follow the example given below.

Example: s̲iːt̲

(a) __ ɪ __	(b) __ ɒ __	(c) __ uː __	(d) __ ɜː __	(e) __ e __
(f) __ ɔː __	(g) __ ʌ __	(h) __ æ __	(i) __ ɪ __	(j) __ ʊ __
(k) __ uː __	(l) __ uː __	(m) __ æ __	(n) __ ɪ __	(o) __ æ __
(p) __ iː __	(q) __ aɪ __	(r) __ eɪ __	(s) __ ɔɪ __	(t) __ eɪ __

Task 3

Listen to the following words on the CD and underline the letter(s) which represent the given symbol. Follow the example below. Refer to the appendix to check your answers.

Example ***symbol:*** /θ/ ***word:*** th̲umb

s.no.	symbol	word
a.	/dʒ/	courage
b.	/ʃ/	pressure
c.	/ð/	that
d.	/ŋ/	bring
e.	/z/	size
f.	/ʒ/	treasure
g.	/dʒ/	suggest
h.	/m/	plumber
i.	/k/	pocket
j.	/g/	beggar
k.	/tʃ/	catch
l.	/n/	knee

m.	/f/	rough
n.	/θ/	thought
o.	/z/	scissors
p.	/ʃ/	conscious
q.	/ʒ/	division
r.	/r/	rhyme
s.	/f/	graph
t.	/ʃ/	machine
u.	/s/	descend
v.	/z/	reason
w.	/ʃ/	sugar
x.	/ð/	weather
y.	/j/	new
z.	/w/	language
a1.	/r/	wrong
b1.	/h/	whole
c1.	/j/	value
d1.	/z/	exact

TASK 4

Listen to each of the following words. Write down the symbols for the consonants in each word, and put a dash(–) for the vowel/s as in the example below.

Example ***small: /sm _____ l/***

(a) throw	(b) quick	(c) think	(d) mix	(e) puncture
(f) ocean	(g) laugh	(h) trophy	(i) bank	(j) severe
(k) desert	(l) essay	(m) lodge	(n) soldier	(o) hammer
(p) tugged	(q) text	(r) flash	(s) cement	(t) buzz
(u) streams	(v) locked	(w) snout	(x) ball	(y) schedule

APPENDIX C

THE VOWELS OF ENGLISH

ACTIVITY

Listen to the vowel sounds of English on the CD, look at the symbols that represent them and repeat the key words.

s.no.	phonetic symbol	key words
a.	/iː/	eat, greet, tea
b.	/ɪ/*	in, skin, bid
c.	/e/	end, guest, said
d.	/æ/	add, plait, span
e.	/ɑː/	ask, balm, star
f.	/ɒ/	on, cough, what
g.	/ɔː/	all, board, sword pour
h.	/ʊ/**	push, wool, should
i.	/uː/	food, group, blue, crew
j.	/ʌ/	up, onion, flood, tough
k.	/ɜː/	earth, serve, first, worse
l.	/ə/	alike, upon, forget, letter
m.	/eɪ/	aid, weight, say
n.	/əʊ/	own, mould, sew
o.	/aɪ/	ice, rhyme, dye
p.	/ɔɪ/	oil, coin, toy

* Note: Advanced Learner's Dictionary (7th edition) lists another vowel symbol /i/. This does not need to be learnt because in its place we can use /ɪ/.

** Note: Advanced Learner's Dictionary (7th edition) lists another vowel symbol /u/. This does not need to be learnt because in its place we can use /ʊ/.

q.	/aʊ/	owl, mouth, now
r.	/ɪə/	ear, fierce, here
s.	/eə/	air, scarce, bear
t.	/ʊə/	tour, rural, gourd, pure

TASK 1

Listen carefully to the following words on the CD and fill in the blank space in each of them with the symbol for the vowel you hear. Refer to the appendix to check your answers.

Example: **said: /sed/**

(a) b — t (b) b — t (c) b — t (d) b — t (e) b — t (f) b — t
(g) b — t (h) b — t (i) b — t (j) b — t (k) b — t

TASK 2

Listen to the following words and fill in the blank space in each of them with the symbol for the vowel you hear. Refer to the appendix to check your answers.

(a) h — d (b) h — d (c) h — d (d) h — d (e) h — d
(f) h — d (g) h — d (h) h — d (i) h — d

TASK 3

Listen to the following words and fill in the blank space in each with symbol numbers (m) to (t) in the list of vowels on page 9. Refer to the appendix to check your answers.

(a) kr — d (b) p — s (c) v — s (d) b — (e) w — (f) dj — l
(g) kl — (h) st — z (i) θ — rɪ (j) sl — t (k) k — m (l) v — l

TASK 4

In the following words, underline the letters that represent the given vowel symbol. After you finish, take turns with a partner to say each of the words aloud.

Example: **symbol /u:/ word** cool

s.no.	symbol	word
a.	/uː/	rude
b.	/ɪə/	pierce
c.	/ʌ/	trouble
d.	/ə/	famous
e.	/aɪ/	island
f.	/əʊ/	bowl
g.	/iː/	people
h.	/ɑː/	aunt
i.	/ʊ/	wolf
j.	/eɪ/	straight
k.	/ɔː/	thought
l.	/ɜː/	journey
m.	/ɒ/	because
n.	/e/	leopard
o.	/ɪ/	sieve
p.	/eə/	various
q.	/ʊə/	truant

TASK 5

Turn to the words in task 4 of unit 2. Look at each word, listen to it once again and fill in the blanks in the words with the symbol for the vowel you hear. The first word is given below as an example. After you finish, refer to the appendix to check your answers.

***Example:* /θrəʊ/**

TASK 6

Listen to the following words and write down the vowel sounds represented by the underlined letters. Take turns with your partner to say each of the words aloud.

(a) priest (b) curry (c) flute (d) beard (e) flood
(f) learn (g) afraid (h) China (i) rural (j) period
(k) folk (l) rhyme (m) hilarious (n) subject (o) oven
(p) bargain (q) serious (r) build (s) claim (t) guest

TASK 7

Transcribe each of the words in task 6 above, and check your transcription with the one given in the dictionary. Say the transcribed words aloud again.

APPENDIX D

THE RELATIONSHIP BETWEEN SPELLING AND SOUND

Useful points to remember

1. *Silent Letters*

   As we said earlier, there is no one-to-one correspondence between spelling and sound. One of the differences between these is silent letters. Let us look at spelling sequences in which there are silent letters.

   a. In the spelling sequence *gh*, the letter *h* is silent. In the word final position *h* is silent:

spelling	pronunciation	spelling	pronunciation
ghost	/gəust/	ah	/ɑː/
aghast	/əgɑːst/	oh	/əʊ/
ghastly	/gɑːstlɪ/	eh	/eɪ/
ghetto	/getəʊ/		

   The letter *h* is also silent in the proper nouns 'John', 'Thames' and 'Thomas'.

   b. In the spelling sequences *mb* and *bt*, the *b* is always silent when it comes in the final position in words.

spelling	pronunciation
limb	/lɪm/
comb	/kəʊm/
lamb	/læm/
tomb	/tuːm/
bomb	/bɒm/

womb	/wu:m/
thumb	/θʌm/
climb	/klaɪm/
doubt	/daʊt/
debt	/det/

The letter *b* is also silent in 'plumber', 'bomber' and 'subtle'.

c. The letter *k* is silent in the sequence *kn* when it comes in the initial position in words.

spelling	pronunciation	spelling	pronunciation
knee	/ni:/	knight	/naɪt/
knob	/nɒb/	knowledge	/nɒlɪdʒ/
knife	/naɪf/	kneel	/ni:l/

d. When the sequence of letters *lk* and *lm* come at the end of a word, the letter *l* is silent.

spelling	pronunciation	spelling	pronunciation
talk	/tɔ:k/	balm	/bɑ:m/
folk	/fəʊk/	palm	/pɑ:m/
stalk	/stɔ:k/	calm	/cɑ:m/
walk	/wɔ:k/		

e. In the spelling sequence *dj*, *d* is silent.

spelling	pronunciation
adjective	/ædʒɪktɪv/
adjudge	/ədʒʌdʒ/
adjust	/ədʒʌst/
adjoin	/ədʒɔɪn/
adjourn	/ədʒɜ:n/
adjacent	/ədʒeɪsənt/

f. The letter *n* is silent in the word-final sequence *mn*.

spelling	pronunciation
autumn	/ɔːtəm/
column	/kɒləm/
condemn	/kəndem/
damn	/dæm/
hymn	/hɪm/
solemn	/sɒləm/

g. The letter *g* is silent in the spelling sequence *gm* or *gn*.

spelling	pronunciation
phlegm	/flem/
paradigm	/pærədaɪm/
gnash	/næʃ/
gnat	/næt/
gnaw	/nɔː/
champagne	/ʃæmpeɪn/
poignant	/pɔɪnjənt/
physiognomy	/fɪzɪɒnəmɪ/
sign	/saɪn/
resign	/rɪzaɪn/
assign	/əsaɪn/
malign	/məlaɪn/
campaign	/kæmpeɪn/

h. The letter *w* is silent in the final position in words.

spelling	pronunciation
bow(vb)	/baʊ/
claw	/klɔː/
blow	/bləʊ/
flow	/fləʊ/
show	/ʃəʊ/
snow	/snəʊ/

i. The letter *w* is silent in *wr* when it comes in word-initial position.

spelling	pronunciation
wring	/rɪŋ/
write	/raɪt/
wrist	/rɪst/
wrap	/ræp/
wreck	/rek/

j. The letter *w* is silent in the following *wh* word-initial sequences.

spelling	pronunciation
who	/hu:/
whom	/hu:m/
whose	/hu:z/
whole	/həul/

k. The letter *t* is silent when it occurs between *s* and *l*.

spelling	pronunciation
castle	/kɑ:s^{ə}l*/
bristle	/brɪs^{ə}l/
apostle	/əpɒs^{ə}l/
whistle	/wɪs^{ə}l/

l. The letter *t* is silent when it occurs between *s* and *en*.

spelling	pronunciation
fasten	/fɑ:s^{ə}n/
listen	/lɪs^{ə}n/
glisten	/glɪs^{ə}n/

2. *Double Consonant Letters*

All double consonant letters except *cc* are pronounced as single consonant sounds, e.g. 'hammer' /hæmə/, 'summer' /sʌmə/ and 'rubber' /rʌbə/. The double letters *cc* are pronounced /k/ in some cases. For example: 'accord', 'account', 'occupy', 'occasion', 'accurate' and accompany. In other cases

* The symbol 'ə' placed above the line as superscript indicates that the sound is optional.

the letters *cc* are pronounced /ks/. For example, 'accede', 'accent', 'accept', 'success', 'access' and 'accelerate'.

3. *Pronunciation of plural forms of words*

   The plural forms of words, ending in *-s*, *-es* and *-ies*, are pronounced as follows:

   a. /ɪz/ after the consonant sounds /s, z, ʃ, ʒ, tʃ, dʒ/. For example, 'buses', 'bushes', 'garages', 'watches', 'bridges', 'roses'.
   b. /s/ after the consonant sounds /p, t, k, f, θ/. For example, 'stops', 'cats', 'parks', 'chiefs' and 'hearths'.
   c. /z/ after all other consonants and all vowels. For example, 'bags', 'tubs', 'buds', 'buns', 'sums', 'stalls', 'songs', 'groves', 'plays', 'toys', 'cars', 'fleas' and 'flies'.

4. *Pronunciation of the past tense forms of verbs*

   The past tense form of words ending in *-ed*, *-d* and *-ied* is pronounced as follows:

   a. /ɪd/ after the consonant sounds /t, d/. For example:

parted	raided
sorted	hounded
wanted	plodded
batted	

   b. /t/ after the consonant sounds /p, k, tʃ, f, θ, s, ʃ/. For example:

tapped	earthed
looked	ceased
watched	brushed
laughed	

   c. /d/ after all other consonant and all vowel sounds. For example:

rubbed	starved
dragged	called
plunged	dried
hummed	prayed
signed	bathed
banged	agreed

ACTIVITY 1

Listen to all the words in 4 (a), (b) and (c) and repeat them for practice.

5. *Pronunciation of the letter sequence ng*

a. The letters *ng* are pronounced /ŋ/ in the word-final position. For example:

bring	running
song	hitting
wrong	filling
thing	keeping

b. In the word-medial position, *ng* is pronounced /ŋ/ in words formed from other words ending in /ŋ/. For example:

singer	singing	things	cuttings
hanger	flings	sings	fillings
ringing	brings	hangman	

c. In all other cases, *ng* is pronounced /ŋg/. For example:

finger	hunger
longer	stronger
anger	

ACTIVITY 2

Listen to each word in section 5 (a), (b) and (c) and repeat it for practice.

ANSWER KEY

APPENDIX A

TASK 1

a. *Pairs of words that are pronounced alike:*
sail – sale, rain – reign, weather – whether, heard – herd, wrap – rap, suite – sweet, piece – peace, pane – pain

TASK 2

	word	number of letters	number of sounds
a.	curry	5	4
b.	sign	4	3
c.	box	3	4
d.	common	6	5
e.	live	4	3
f.	pretty	6	5
g.	exact	5	6
h.	bead	4	3
i.	quick	5	4
j.	wrong	5	3
k.	kitchen	7	5
l.	college	7	5
m.	friend	6	5
n.	funny	5	4
o.	bridge	6	4

TASK 3

a. right b. strait c. might d. son e. bough
f. bare g. tale h. caste i. site j. role.

TASK 4

(a) knight (b) calm (c) comb (d) adjective (e) adjust
(f) resign (g) gnat (h) walk (i) column (j) solemn
(k) folk (l) pneumonia (m) castle (n) almond (o) listen
(p) whole (q) whose (r) wrist (s) doubt (t) receipt

APPENDIX B

TASK 1

(a) /ʃ/ (b) /v/ (c) /m/ (d) /tʃ/ (e) /g/ (f) /ʒ/ (g) /z/
(h) /dʒ/ (i) /w/ (j) /h/ (k) /ð/ (l) /ŋ/ (m) /f/ (n) /θ/
(o) /j/ (p) /p/ (q) /r/ (r) /ʒ/ (s) /ð/ (t) /dʒ/ (u) /z/

TASK 2

(a) /gɪv/ (b) /ʃɒk/ (c) /ruːd/ (d) /hɜːb/ (e) /dʒet/
(f) /sɔːd/ (g) /θʌm/ (h) /dʒæm/ (i) /sɪŋ/ (j) /pʊf/
(k) /jʊːθ/ (l) /fuːd/ (m) /kætʃ/ (n) /zɪp/ (o) /bædʒ/
(q) /ðiːz/ (r) /tʃaɪm/ (s) /ʃeɪp/ (t) /vɔɪs/ (u) /beɪʒ/

TASK 3

courage, pressure, that, bring, size, treasure, suggest, plumber, pocket, beggar, catch, knee, rough, thought, scissors, conscious, division, rhyme, graph, machine, descend, reason, sugar, weather, new, language, wrong, whole, value, exact

TASK 4

(a) θr — (b) kw — k (c) θ — ŋk (d) m — ks
(e) p — ŋktʃ — (f) — ʃn (g) l — f (h) tr — f —
(i) b — ŋk (j) s — v — (k) d — z — t (l) — s —
(m) l — dʒ (n) s — ldʒ — (o) h — m — (p) t — gd
(q) t — kst (r) fl — ʃ (s) s — m — nt (t) b — z
(u) str — mz (v) l — kt (w) sn — t (x) b — l
(y) ʃ — dj — l

APPENDIX C

TASK 1

(a) /e/ (b) /ɔː/ (c) /æ/ (d) /iː/ (e) /uː/ (f) /ɪ/
(g) /aʊ/ (h) /aɪ/ (i) /əʊ/ (j) /eɪ/ (k) /ʌ/

TASK 2

(a) /aɪ/ (b) /æ/ (c) /iː/ (d) /ɑː/ (e) /ɔː/ (f) /e/ (g) /ʊ/ (h) /ɪ/ (i) /ɜː/

TASK 3

(a) /aʊ/ (b) /eɪ/ (c) /ɔɪ/ (d) /aʊ/ (e) /eə/ (f) /ʊə/
(g) /ɪə/ (h) /eə/ (i) /ɪə/ (j) /aɪ/ (k) /əʊ/ (l) /eɪ/

TASK 4

r<u>u</u>de, p<u>ie</u>rce, tr<u>ou</u>ble, fam<u>ou</u>s, <u>is</u>land, b<u>ow</u>l, p<u>eo</u>ple, <u>au</u>nt, w<u>o</u>lf, str<u>aigh</u>t, th<u>ough</u>t, j<u>our</u>ney, bec<u>au</u>se, l<u>eo</u>pard, s<u>ie</u>ve, v<u>a</u>rious, tr<u>ua</u>nt

TASK 5

(a) /θrəu/ (b) /kwɪk/ (c) /θɪŋk/ (d) /mɪks/ (e) /pʌŋktʃə/
(f) /əuʃn/ (g) /lɑːf/ (h) /trəufɪ/ (i) /bæŋk/ (j) /sɪvɪə/
(k) /dezət/ (l) /eseɪ/ (m) /lɒdʒ/ (n) /səuldʒə/ (o) /hæmə/
(p) /tʌgd/ (q) /tekst/ (r) /flæʃ/ (s) /sɪment/ (t) /bʌz/
(u) /striːmz/ (v) /lɒkt/ (w) /snaʊt/ (x) /bɔːl/ (y) /ʃedjuːl/

TASK 6

(a) /iː/ (b) /ʌ/ (c) /uː/ (d) /ɪə/ (e) /ʌ/
(f) /ɜː/ (g) /eɪ/ (h) /aɪ/ (i) /ʊə/ (k) /ɪə/
(l) /əʊ/ (m) /aɪ/ (n) /eə/ (o) /ʌ, ɪ/ (p) /ʌ/
(q) /ɪ/ (r) /ɪə/ (s) /ɪ/ (t) /eɪ/ (u) /e/